Tommy Cornstalk
by

J. H. M. (John Henry McCartney) Abbott

Tommy Cornstalk
Being Some Account of the Less Notable Features of the South
African War From the Point of View of the Australian Ranks

1902

Tommy Cornstalk

John Henry McCartney Abbott

THE SONG OF THE DEAD

Oh, Land of Ours, hear the song we make for you —
Land of yellow wattle bloom, land of smiling Spring —
Hearken to the after words, land of pleasant memories,
Shea-oaks of the shady creeks, hear the song we sing.
For we lie quietly, underneath the stony kops,
Where the Veldt is silent, where the guns have ceased to boom.
Here we are waiting, and shall wait to Eternity —
Here on the battle-fields, where we have found our doom.

Spare not thy pity — Life is strong and fair for you —
City by the waterside, homestead on the plain.
Keep ye remembrance, keep ye a place for us —
So all the bitterness of dying be not vain.
Oh, be ye mindful, mindful of our honour's name;
Oh, be ye careful of the word ye speak in jest —
For we have bled for you; for we have died for you —
Yea, we have given, we have given of our best.

Life that we might have lived, love that we might have loved,
Sorrow of all sorrows, we have drunk thy bitter lees.
Speak thou a word to us, here in our narrow beds —
Word of thy mourning in lands beyond the Seas.
Lo, we have paid the price, paid the cost of Victory.
Do not forget, when the rest shall homeward come —
Mother of our childhood, sister of our manhood's days,
Loved of our heavy hearts, whom we have left alone.

Hark to the guns — pause, and turn, and think of us —
Red was our life's blood, and heavy was the cost.
But ye have Nationhood, but ye are a people strong —
Oh, have ye love for the brothers ye have lost?
Oh, — by the blue skies, clear beyond the mountain tops,
Oh, by the dear, dun plains where we were bred, —
What be your tokens, tokens that ye grieve for us,
Tokens of your Sorrowing for me that be Dead?

TO THE MEMORY OF
W. R. H.
KILLED IN ACTION AT
DIAMOND HILL
JUNE 12, 1900
This book is affectionately dedicated

PREFACE

To so great an extent has the market been flooded with all sorts and conditions of books relative to the war in South Africa that the author feels constrained to introduce his with a few words of apology and explanation, in the hope that he may perhaps justify himself for seeking to inflict yet another upon a long-suffering public.

War Correspondents, Doctors, Members of Parliament, Lords and Lookers-on have, all and sundry, had their say in book form as to what they have seen and what they have thought about it. Battles, strategy, transport, hospitals—all the varied features of both campaigns have been most thoroughly discussed and debated in their diversity of light and shade from almost every possible point of view. So that there would seem at first very little left to write about. But the Australian soldier, though frequently the subject of much literary effort, has not yet had his say. Therefore, in these pages the author has striven to show other Australians, who had not the good fortune to serve in Africa, what some phases of campaigning were like, as viewed from the standpoint of the Australian ranks, and has occasionally ventured to say, as an Australian, how things have impressed him.

With regard to the two "Battle" chapters, it is perhaps necessary to explain that, though the incidents and setting are actual facts, the whole is not intended to represent any particular engagement, but is rather a kind of composite portrait of half a dozen or more.

In conclusion, the author wishes to acknowledge the kindly assistance and advice for which he is indebted to Mr. John Arthur Barry in the making of this book.

SYDNEY, 1902.

CONTENTS

CHAPTER I - THE CORNSTALK

There was a story sent from the Front by the Correspondent of a Sydney daily newspaper, concerning a Great General, a Field Hospital and Geography.

New South Wales had a very well-equipped and well-served Army Medical Corps, which, when troops were offered for service in South Africa by the Australasian Colonies, had despatched two field ambulances to the Cape. One of them was at Paardeberg whilst Cronje sullenly stood at bay in the Modder. The Great General came to see it. Everything was good, and complete, and well done, and of an excellence that does not show through a binding of red tape; and the Great General had never before seen anything quite so good, or complete, or so well done, and was pleased and interested in all he saw.

"Who are you? " he asked, "and where do you come from? " To which the P. M.O. made answer: "We are part of the New South Wales Army Medical Corps".

"Ah, yes, " returned the Great General; "yes, New South Wales! That's Adelaide, isn't it? "

Now the application of this little tale is, that if Great Generals do not know that New South Wales is not a suburb of Adelaide, how much less will the average un-Australian reader comprehend the meaning of the term 'Cornstalk'?

In Gippsland grow the big gum trees. It is a matter of some pride, perhaps, to Victorians that their province should grow the largest gum trees in all the Australias. Jealous of Victorian prowess in eucalyptus cultivation, so to speak, the other Australians refer to the Victorian people collectively as 'Gum-suckers'!

Because the popular banana finds the climate of Queensland suitable to its healthy being, the inhabitants of that Colony are dubbed 'Banana-landers'.

It may have been that, to the early South Australians, means of subsistence came not easily. At any rate they are called 'Crow-eaters'.

In delicate reference to the nature of their country the West Australians are 'Sand-gropers'.

Finally, the people of New South Wales, having acquired a reputation for lankiness and wiriness, have been named 'Cornstalks'.

That a native of the mother colony differs very greatly from the human product of any other part of Australia is possibly doubtful, but that, in the days of his youth at any rate, he is usually slimly built and long of limb is a fact fairly well established. See him in his own country—along the creeks and rivers of the eastern ranges, on the New England and Monaro tablelands, or out in the sun-baked West—and you will find that there is something about him peculiarly characteristic, something of his own that marks him slightly, but still unmistakably, as himself and no one else. Place the average bush-bred boy of eighteen beside the same aged English lad and note the difference.

The Cornstalk is the almost immediate successor of the Hawkesbury native—is indeed symbolical of the evolution of that physically perfect being. Years ago, we of the present generation are told, if you should see anywhere a particularly tall, brawny, well-made, big man, you might be morally certain that he hailed from the farms upon the Hawkesbury River flats. The first of the free settlers who commenced the march westwards 'squatted' there, and owned the land by right of occupation. If they could obtain them, they took wives unto themselves, and reared up families. And the families subsisted principally upon pumpkin and ground maize, and wore no boots in their childhood, and led a free, wild, untrammelled sort of life. So they grew into tall, clean-limbed, deep-chested men, and sturdy, comely women, and spread North and West and South over the land—and their offspring were the fathers and mothers of the Cornstalks of to-day.

There were, of course, other places besides the banks of the Hawkesbury where the pioneers tilled the land and grazed their flocks, but the Hawkesbury native is typical of the best men and women of that time.

Big and large, the Cornstalk is a good man. Like most other good men, he has his faults—even his vices—but they are not yet the faults and vices that bring a people to the gutter. His is not a new race—it is rather the renewed, reinvigorated reproduction of an older one.

Tommy Cornstalk

He has the blemishes of his forebears, the transmitted characteristics of a not too perfect ancestry. He has developed little traits, and big traits, of his own; and many of his leanings look alarming. But, even now, there is promise and hope—and, if we may be permitted to say it of one's own people—some fulfilment.

He has been spoken of in the Literature of the Hopeless as 'tired'. He has been painted as a somewhat weary decadent—too listless, too blasé, too worn-down by the overwhelming burden of existence to act the part of a strong man, of a vigorous and energetic citizen. The weird melancholy of the Bush has warped his soul. Too much meat, too much tobacco, too little grinding poverty, have combined to unnerve and render him effete. If we are to believe it all, he is tending towards a sort of demoralising apathy, a listless carelessness that will make him, in time, something akin to the more degenerate Latin type—a creature too feeble, too vacillating and uncertain, to help himself and keep his place near the surface in the struggle for existence. But, perhaps, recent events have proved that this is a false view. We may thank Heaven that he is better than he has been represented to be in this class of literature.

He is, at times, 'flash'. He considers himself to be rather a better man than most other men. He is said to lack reverential feeling, to respect little that is worthy of respect. Undoubtedly he loves holiday, he thinks more of sport than of work. He is well able to sound his own trumpet, and he thoroughly believes in the correctness of its notes. But these are not hopeless characteristics. Flashness is only another name for self-confidence—merely the over development of the bump of self-respect. It is good and healthy to appreciate oneself. He does not really want in reverence—he is shy. Why should he not love sport and holiday? Few of us work for fun, and if you don't sound your own trumpet, who is likely to sound it for you? Taking him 'in the lump, ' the Cornstalk is not a bad fellow. Above all things, he is no Degenerate.

Curiously noticeable in South Africa were the variations in 'English as she is spoke' amongst the troops of the Empire. From the broad dialects of the men from the different counties of England—of the Scotch and of the Irish—the speech and accent of the various Colonial contingents were strangely distinct. To the newcomer from Canada or Australia, a Yorkshire 'Tommy' was, at first, almost as unintelligible as a Chinaman. Doubtless the reverse was true also. There were few distinctions in dress as the campaign grew older, and most men looked alike, but one was generally able to locate a man's habitat in the Empire as soon as he opened his lips to speak. From the rounded, full-voiced English, the broad Scotch, or the Irish brogue, the Canadian twang and the Australian drawl were as distinguishable as the French language is from the German. Roughly, the difference is this—the Englishman says all his word; the Canadian emphasises the last syllable sharply, and the Australian slurs the terminations. In Australia, where all people speak more or less alike, this peculiarity of ours escapes one; but in Africa, where it could be compared, and always was in contrast, with so many accents and modes of expression, it was extraordinarily apparent. And of nothing was this difference in speech more suggestive than of the wideness of the Empire.

So Tommy Cornstalk is generally a long-limbed fellow, with a drawling twang, to whom anything in the nature of sport appeals most strongly. He is a newer being than the English 'Tommy, ' and he is pretty much, though not quite, of the same species as the Canadian.

But we want to consider him as a soldier, and to discover what his capacities and capabilities are for soldiering.

Above, of course, one has not considered the Cornstalk of the city. His is another story. The Cockney is not taken as the standard Englishman. John Bull is typically a farmer; and his son Jack Bull, of Australia, is a bushman.

Most of the rank and file of the troops who went to South Africa from Australia were of the Bush.

From the history of the Dutch people in South Africa—their hardships and struggles as pioneers in the first place, and their open-air, half-civilised existence nowadays—it was, from the outbreak of hostilities, a matter of universal opinion throughout the Colonies that the Boer should be met by men who resembled him in their ways of living, in their training as horsemen, and, more particularly, in their education as expert rifle shots.

When troops were offered by the several Australian Governments last year (and accepted perhaps in the first place as a compliment), the movement was regarded in Australia not as a mere formal evidencing of the loyalty and good will of the Colonies to the

Motherland, but rather as a serious step taken to assist her with men trained to the same conditions, if not of war, then of ordinary life as obtain amongst the Veldt-dwelling Boers of South Africa. And, afterwards, the Imperial Government seemed to view the matter in the same light; though at first, before the irregular troops had proved that they were of some worth, at least, there seemed to be in England the feeling of 'we-don't-want-them-but-they'll-feel-hurt-if-we-refuse'.

The Bushman—the dweller in the country as opposed to the town-abiding folk—the real Cornstalk, is, to all practical purposes, of the same kind as the Boer. It is not to be supposed for a moment that he generally possesses the meaner attributes of the Boer character. He is not constitutionally a liar (except in the matters of horses and dogs). However one may wish to do the Africander justice, it is difficult to believe that he possesses the same views with regard to honour and fair dealing as obtain amongst Englishmen. To be 'slim, ' to 'verneuk' his neighbour, is, with the Boer, a by no means bad failing. We are certainly no better in most things than we ought to be, but, if only as policy, we do deal more with truthfulness than do the Boers.

One does not wish to decry or make little of a people whom one has learned to respect as a brave and hardy race, and a gallant foe, and it is perhaps the most charitable view to take if we assume that the Boer's ready resort to lying of a bad kind is a flaw in his nature for which he is scarcely accountable—and try and understand that he is sometimes unable to grasp the wrongness of falsity and crooked dealing. It is not intended, therefore, to imply that the Cornstalk, when likened to the Boer, is necessarily possessed of the more objectionable attributes of the latter. Neither, moreover, is he such a slothful and retrogressive person in his conduct of life. What we wish to point out is, that in training, in conditions of living, in environment, and to some extent in ancestry, the Cornstalk and the Boer have very much that is in common.

As a soldier, Tommy Cornstalk differs considerably from his cousin Tommy Atkins. His soldiering is mainly of the present. Active service is the first occasion upon which he has been called to obey unquestioningly in all things since he has worn a uniform. The only discipline he really knows is the 'discipline of enthusiasm'. He may have made many sacrifices for his volunteering. He may have been accustomed to ride miles to his parades. His shooting may have cost him time and money. He may have taken pains innumerable to perfect himself, as far as was in his power, and with the means at his command, in all his duties—but, until he has signed his attestation paper, almost until he has embarked upon the troopship, he has never thoroughly been 'under the whip'! He has never known what it means to be the unthinking piece of mechanism, the pawn in the game, which all soldiers necessarily become under a strict and unswerving discipline.

And, at first, he does not take altogether kindly to it. He has been a free man—within certain limits a law unto himself—accustomed in his democratic country to acknowledge no man as being, per se, his superior, unless a well-tested one. He may have been to school with some of his officers, may know them intimately in civil life. It is even possible that, in his own district, he may occupy a social position above that of his officer. And this is where, to the average Cornstalk soldier, the shoe pinches. It seems to him bitterly hard that he is required to salute a man whom he may not consider at all his better. It is irk-some and uncongenial to him to have to address him as 'Sir, ' or as 'Mister So-and-so'. It is absurd to be expected to stand 'as stiff as a gate post' with his toes nicely turned out to an angle of forty-five degrees. It annoys him to have to trouble himself about the paying of compliments and such like, to his thinking, vexatious and foolish matters. And so, when he meets the Imperial Officer he astonishes him; and when he meets Tommy Atkins he wins that gentleman's admiration and awestruck regard by his cool and happy neglect of the things which have been drilled into Tommy as sacredly to be observed under all circumstances.

"What is the use of it all? " he argues; "how does it help to lick the Boers, and get to Pretoria? "

As the Boer despises a 'voet-looper' so is Tommy Cornstalk ashamed to be seen walking. He is essentially a horseman—and generally a horsey man. His sphere as a soldier lies in mounted work—rather, perhaps, in the work of mounted infantry than in that of cavalry. To be a 'toey' seems to him almost to amount to degradation. He thanks God that he is not an infantryman—and this not because he does not give credit for and respect the magnificent work of the infantry, but because it is his nature to look down upon the man who walks. In Australia the possession of a horse carries with it something of a guarantee of respectability and solvency. A man who cannot read is far less to be pitied than one who cannot ride.

Generally, he is a good shot. Indeed, it is doubtful whether there is any better shot in the world than the kangaroo-shooter—although, of course, all Cornstalks are not kangaroo-shooters. He is quite as good, if not a slightly better shot than the Boer. But he must fire as he pleases. Volleys, save when delivered at long and uncertain ranges to keep down the fire of the enemy, find small favour with him. It is not enough for him to 'loose off' his rifle, in the vague hope of his bullet chancing to drop where some one is; he must have a definite target to 'loose off' at.

Whatever Tommy Cornstalk may be as a fighter, he owes little of his capacity for war to drill or instruction. He has known no riding-school, he has not studied the care of the horse in a little red book. It is only by painful effort that he learns to roll his coat correctly over his wallet—in order that he may give his mount a sore wither. He would prefer to carry it in a fashion less uncomfortable for his horse. He is feeble in the salute. He hardly ever knows when to turn out the guard. His concerted movements lack precision. He resents exclusiveness—even in a General Officer.

But nevertheless he is a highly trained man of war. He has learned to ride through pine scrubs, down mountain sides, over rotten ground, about cattle camps. It has been his business to be a horseman. He has been more or less of a horseman from his babyhood. He has studied marching on the travelling stock routes; to endure thirst on the dry stages; to sleep in the mud or the saddle. Mother Earth is a familiar bed. His knowledge of scouting has been acquired young. You cannot teach a man to scout in a suburb or from a text-book. To look for sheep across a plain that quivers with mirage, or upon the steep 'sidings' in the hills, to seek wild cattle in the scrubs, trains one's eyes. Tracks acquire a language when a knowledge of their 'true inwardness' may mean your daily bread.

He has been taught to forage on the road. The feeding of one horse in war time is a simple matter compared to stealing grass for a mob of sheep or cattle. He has had to cook for himself, to sew for himself, to depend upon himself in his often lonely, self-reliant existence. In his own business, his daily life, he has unconsciously been taught what is as important a thing to know on active service as anything (and which all the barrack training of the regular will not have taught him), and that is how to be comfortable, how to become a good 'doer' under all adverse circumstances.

'Looting' comes to him naturally, though apparently not quite so naturally as to the Canadian, who is the most accomplished 'looter' in all the world.

This is a compliment which is none the less deserved because all looting was sternly forbidden by the British authorities; and as it happened, therefore, neither Cornstalk nor Canadian had much scope for the exercise of this particular talent.

Except for the fact that it is treeless, the veldt is not unlike our plain country. It is better watered, and often better grassed.

But, altogether, the Cornstalk was at home in it. There were the same long distances between towns. The 'dorp' represented the Bush township. There were the familiar wire fences. The sky above was as darkly blue. There was, as a rule, plenty of sunshine, and the wide rolling downs quivered and danced with the same beautiful mirage-making islands of kopjes, and long, low spits of ridges. He had to fight in a country not altogether so new to him as it must have been to Englishmen.

CHAPTER II - THE VELDT

Writing in the Friend at Bloemfontein, during the short but brilliant existence of that journal as a 'commandeered' newspaper, under the editorial direction of several of the war correspondents, a contributor described the veldt as 'inexpressible'. And, if you come to think of it, that is just about what it is.

Lonely, mournful, wild, mysterious—all the adjectives you may care to lavish upon it, and something besides that you are not able to say. There is some key-note to it all which is hard to find—something subtle, vague, half-hidden. Lonely it is; terribly lonely in its great distances, its broad stretches of level plain, or rolling downs, without habitation. Mysterious, in its mile upon mile of changeless characteristic, its very duplication of itself. Mournful, in its apparent emptiness of most that makes a country prosperous. Wild, in its half-savage black population, and its almost as half-savage white one. It is beautiful or hideous, sad or bright in the sunshine, as the mood takes you, but always, even unto the worst of its recollection, it is fascinating, and fascinating because it is inexpressible.

You may have starved on it, shivered in wet blankets as you lay in its clinging mud, bled on it, buried your comrade in it—but afterwards, when you look back to it, and time shall have wrapped a haze of interest round its sterner outlines, you will remember the charm, the half-unconscious attractiveness, the indefinable something that was of its very nature. At any rate, you will never forget it.

Sunrise—with dew sparkling like diamond points on the long waving grass, the fresh breeze fanning your face, the glorious blue sky overhead boasting of the coming day, the flat-topped purple kopjes far away on the yellow horizon; a white farmhouse, with its deep green setting of eucalyptus and willow, in the middle distance; and the splendid, dry, invigorating atmosphere about you—was always beautiful. In the noontide, the clear sunlight made lakes and lagoons before you, clearer and more distinct even than the mirage of our Western plains. In the evening, the sunset threw long shadows of men and horses across the long levels. And at night, when you lay out on its wide bosom, tucked away snugly into your brown blanket—the bright stars glittering like electric points up in their indigo setting, while the smoke from your pipe curled lazily into the darkness, and you thanked God for a few hours of rest and peace—then it was that the veldt had its greatest charm.

It might easily have been that one had to muster Sandy Flat or the Black Mountain in the morning. There might have been branding to start on in the daylight, or forty miles to ride through the pine scrub and belar before you should camp again. In the drowsy interval between the last few whiffs of Boer tobacco and sleep, it was not very difficult to imagine oneself spending a night out on the Run, with prospect of a hard day's work to be done on the morrow.

But it was only then, in the dreamy state before oblivion, that you could think such things. All round were the far-stretching lines of picketed horses, looming black and indistinct in the faint light from sparse and tiny fires; the crouching figures of overcoated men cooking their scanty rations for next day's march, and huddled heaps of sleepers between the horse lines.

And if, later, you should awake when the precious fires had dwindled down to points of light, and only the sentries on the lines sat shivering in the early morning chill, you would find something wanting in the veldt-night, something whose absence would strike you as strangely unfamiliar in your experience of sleeping out o' doors. Everything seemed to have become quiet. There were no crickets, no frogs, no ''possums' scratching in the trees, no curlews with their wailing notes, no plover—nothing but dead absolute silence—save the muffled munching of an occasional hungry horse nibbling at the grass beside his picket-leg.

Now, in the Bush there is never silence, comparatively; everything is quiet and at rest, but all night long you hear the subdued hum of wakeful life of some kind—the ceaseless chirping of crickets, the hoot of a mophawk or a night owl, the wild discordant screech of plover, a frog croaking unweariedly in the creek below you, a 'willy-wagtail' trilling his sweet notes in the tree overhead—always some performer in Nature's orchestra playing his little part in the ceaseless symphony of night.

But here, in this naked Africa, everything is stiller than the grave at night. Once, may-be, you might have lain awake and heard the beasts come down to water, and the lions roaring, but now the lions are in the North—none nearer than the Zoutpansberg—and the buck are scared away too far by the presence of all these men and horses to disturb your rest by nocturnal wanderings. And it is this uncanny stillness that reminds you of the fact that you are not at home in the good Bush. There will be no branding to-morrow. It will be harder work than branding, more exciting rides than chasing cattle through the scrubs or down the mountain tracks. And you are never quite certain whether there will be another nightfall for you. But that doesn't trouble you much. If you can get some biscuits and some bully-beef, and a fairly even place to spread your blanket in, the consideration of eternity may easily postpone itself for the time being.

One day, it came to pass that a 'Rimington Tiger' and the writer foregathered at the back of a battle—the one having been sent upon a message and being unable to find his regiment again, and the other with a dead-lame horse whose leg sinews had been wrenched by a fall into an ant-bear hole. Both were tired, and hungry, and thirsty, and uncertain whither to turn, or what to do in order to reach their own units—so they decided to lunch. The 'Tiger, ' who was of a meek aspect redeemed by strong blue eyes, was the fortunate possessor of a canvas water-bag about three parts full, and a pocketful of broken biscuit; and the writer had a little tea and a very much smaller quantity of sugar. So, some way behind a low ridge, along the crest of which recumbent 'khakis' sputtered ceaselessly with their Lee-Metfords, an economical fire was lit, and fed by little sticks and roots from the scanty bushes which supplied the only wood available, and afterwards, when the flame was strong enough to 'go alone, ' with pieces of dry cow-dung. Little white clouds occasionally formed in the air above the ridge, and then groups and driblets of men came away from the firing-line to a field dressing-station over to our right. We were too absorbed in the contemplation of our almost boiling mess-tin to take much notice.

Suddenly a Boer shell came howling beyond the ridge, and banged up a heap of dust and gravel just short of where our cooking operations were being conducted. Things screamed in the air shrilly, so we concluded that our meal would be more inviting if partaken of in some place where such ill-timed and intrusive interruptions were less likely to inflict themselves upon us. Therefore we moved the can and a fire-stick laboriously to another position, and finished the brew under difficulties. The Boer gunners, for some reason best known to themselves, continued to shell the spot where we had been, probably with an idea that stronger re-inforcements were sheltering behind the ridge. After a meal, less abundant than

11

welcome, the Rimington delivered himself of sundry emphatic opinions concerning his native land.

"The country's no dam good, " he said. "I know it from King William's Town to Bulawayo, and it's not fit for a white man to live in. Y'd like to try ten thousand acres? Well, y're better out of it, by a long chalk. Locusts, rinderpest, scab, fluke, foot-rot! Droughts, floods, fires, fever, that's what it is! Crops! What's the use of crops when there's locusts to eat 'em? Good as Australia? Well, Australia ain't much, then. You take it from me—keep clear of Africa, leave farming to the Kaffirs. Mining's the on'y thing, an' y'haven't a dog's show without capital. Rhodesia's the worst of the lot. The country's no dam good. "

But, in spite of this particular Rimington Guide, himself a native of Cape Colony and obviously a pessimist; in spite of scores of other men who should know, and who have spoken of it in a similar strain; in spite of one's own prejudice against a place where one has enjoyed hardship and danger and discomfort, the writer is still of opinion, however little such opinion may be worth, that the country is good—better far even than the general run of Africanders give it credit for being.

Up to Modder River—when en route to Bloemfontein viâ Paardeberg, Osfontein and Driefontein—the country is disappointing. One cannot speak with any knowledge of the karoo after viewing it from the window of a moving train, however leisurely that train may proceed. (And South African trains do not hurry—especially troop trains.) It looks poor, barren, destitute of herbage, or indeed of anything edible, but there were glimpses of flocks of shorn sheep which were in far from poor condition. Some were almost fat. Their only visible means of support was apparently a small, scrubby bush, growing hardly more than a foot or two in height, and not unlike the species of salt-bush known in Australia as 'cotton-bush'.

But generally, thereabouts, the country is wretchedly inhospitable in appearance. Gradual rocky slopes, broken here and there by kopjes and low ranges of stony hills, stretch up beyond De Aar and past the Orange River, until you reach the Modder. Here, there is at least promise of something better. The plains are level, and the soil more promising, and if the surface had not been churned up into endless dust by an army it might have been grassed.

Before the war, Modder River was a favourite 'watering place, ' whither pic-nic parties and Sunday schools came from Kimberley. In springtime the banks were knee-deep in grass, they said, and aglow with beautiful wild-flowers. Now they were cut up by the numberless tracks of waggons and guns, littered with the impedimenta of a great host, scarred with the marks of recent battle. The pretty cottages of the village were torn and pock-marked by shell and bullet, and the drift itself—the beautiful, lazy, tree-shaded drift—a discoloured bog.

Out from the Modder station, on the road to Jacobsdaal, the long plains seemed more like the veldt one had read of than anything seen hitherto. Beyond Osfontein farm—in the early year, just after the rains—it struck one as being almost the best country one had ever seen.

Miles, and miles, and miles of rolling downs stretched away right up to Bloemfontein. Long, waving, succulent grasses, as good as the best our plains produce. You rode through it with the sensation of riding through a field of ripening wheat. It seemed a pity, almost, that all these thousands of horses should trail through it, trampling it down, and wasting it needlessly. So thick and luxuriant was it that it caught in your stirrup-irons, your scabbard 'swished' through it. When you lay down to sleep at night you were in a little grass-walled enclosure. It seemed like an ideal 'fattening' country. And it never looked better than in the early morning, when the sun had painted it gold-green, and the long shadows of the kopjes lay across it like dark carpets. Sometimes we saw the fattest of fat cattle—but terribly mongrel cattle.

And yet people tell you that it is hard to live here, that farming or grazing do not pay. There is the scab, and the rinderpest, and the fluke; and when you're done with all of them, the locust and the drought.

Heavens! they don't know what drought is. Undoubtedly scab, and rinderpest, and fluke, and locusts are formidable things—when you sit down and look at them. What an utterly hopeless, deadly state a man's soul must be in when he can calmly contemplate a visitation of scab, rinderpest, fluke or locusts as the justly incurred manifestation of God's wrath, with whose course it would be impious to meddle, and the only remedy for which is a casting back for sins committed that may have merited punishment, and a resolve to avoid such errors in the future!

According to the Boer mind, you don't get scab in your flock because you have omitted necessary precautions in your methods of sheep-farming, but because you have perhaps stolen a pair of boots when you visited the dorp at Nachtmaal, or because you didn't attend Nachtmaal, or 'took down' your neighbour over a horse-deal when you did. And it is easy to understand how difficult it would be to bring about any concerted action towards counteracting the effect of such visitations as the aforesaid, or stamping out disease altogether amongst such people.

One can only, of course, speak as a tourist speaks of a country he has run through. One's practical knowledge of the veldt and its products is probably limited to some observance of the value or uselessness of its ant-heaps as 'cover' and such purely warlike uses. But, in the light of common reason, in comparison with what our own pastoralists and farmers have to contend with in Australia, in view of its fertility and natural advantages and rainfall, one cannot altogether accept the veldt as bad country, or as country in which it should be difficult to make both ends meet—not to speak of their overlapping. It is well watered naturally and it has splendid facilities for catching rain in tanks and dams. It is fertile—Kaffirs grow great crops of mealies almost by scratching up the soil with a stick. Had it not been for the excellent grazing that it was nearly always possible to obtain for the cavalry horses in the Free State and the Transvaal it is perhaps no exaggeration to say that the rapid movements of the Cavalry Division would have been impossible.

But more weighty than all in arguing favourably to the veldt is the fact that it has supported so large a savage population as it has done in the past, and does still to a lesser extent. After all, the great test of a country's fertility and value—perhaps the only sure test—lies in the number of human beings and wild animals it will provide a living for.

Perhaps the truest light in which one may regard the veldt is in that of a field that has lain fallow, has never been thoroughly tried, has never yet been given a wholesale chance of showing what it can do.

Considered as a campaigning ground 'much may be said on both sides'. For the defence, the veldt is fortified, and well fortified, by its kopjes. Every kopje is a natural stronghold. But it is too open to really make a stand in, unless it be on the banks of rivers where scrub and brushwood afford 'cover, ' and steep banks shelter from shell-fire. For the attack it ought to be free from possibilities of ambuscade. Unfortunately, it does not seem to have been always so—but that is another story—it should have been. There can be few countries in the world where scouting should be less difficult. Open country, a clear atmosphere, little timber, an almost unavoidable skyline, are natural features that do not readily lend themselves to the concealment of large bodies of men or horses. Consider the difficulties that would present themselves in our veldt country here—the plains. Belts of timber—some kind of cover nearly everywhere—would render the reconnaissance of positions a task of infinitely greater trouble than was the case in the open veldt of South Africa.

Compared, indeed, to almost any part of Australia, the veldt possesses features that render it much less dangerous for the attacker than would be the case here. It is, too, a country where roads may be almost disregarded, and where, consequently, the troubles of transport are very much less than in timbered, hilly, or 'sticky' localities. And, in view of its facilities for grazing, as mentioned above, it was most excellent country from the point of view of the horse, the mule and the ox.

From the domestic standpoint, the veldt was bad—very bad. Its timberless nature was the cause of the greatest hardship that the army had to endure—want of firewood. Sleeping in the open air, even if the weather be wet, is not such a very uncomfortable business, provided that you can obtain a good fire. But when you have no means of cooking the raw beef and flour you sometimes get by way of rations; when you are soaked to the skin, and cannot keep warm; when you have no chance of drying one-half of your body at a time in the glow of a cheerful blaze— then, indeed, is war hard, and stern, and comfortless. Many times did Tommy Cornstalk sigh wearily for just one good ring-barked paddock, for just one big log of the many that were lying all over Australia unappropriated to light his fire under.

On first acquaintance the veldt appears to be an ideal ground for the manoeuvring of mounted troops. Its looks belie it, however, to a certain extent. It is undermined everywhere by holes and burrows of a peculiarly treacherous kind. They were said to be the work of the 'meer-cat' or the 'ant-bear'. Whatever made them, they were always pitfalls for the unwary—and for the wary too. Unless you watched where you were going at the 'trot' or 'gallop, ' you almost always came to grief, and, if you were not damaged yourself, the subsequent state of your horse's leg-sinews generally necessitated your walking for a day or two, or even 'commandeering' from friend or foe, a remount of sorts, according to your skill as a horse-thief, or your luck.

CHAPTER III - THE MARCH

If you have the last couple of hours' 'watch' on the horse-lines, you see it all. The long rows of picketed scarecrows, shivering with drooping heads, each in the little bare circle where he has nibbled the grass to its very roots during the night; the straight rows of saddles in front of the horses; the huddled heaps of brown blankets covering curled-up figures of men in the wet grass; away back in the rear the dingy waggons with the tarpaulins over them, and the cooks' fires in between. It is the half light that makes everything look dull and comfortless just before the fresh new day comes with the promise that seems to wait on every dawn, no matter what the real prospect may be, and, walking up and down to keep warm, you look out on the sleeping camp with a feeling of loneliness and chill.

Already the cooks are astir. You called them half an hour ago—according to your instructions, so that they might make the coffee for breakfast—and they are breaking up biscuit-boxes for fuel, and kindling their fires round the piled up 'dixies' (a 'dixie' is a big cooking pot used for making soup, or tea, or coffee—but why 'dixie' deponent knoweth not). They have been filled overnight, and closely guarded by the cooks, who have slept amongst them, lest unprincipled sinners fill their water-bottles with the precious water they contain, in preparation for the next day's march.

A few Kaffir transport drivers—weird figures crouching in coloured blankets—are boiling their 'mealie-pap' in three-legged pots at little fires of their own.

Across the grey veldt in front, a small cluster of saddled horses, grouped close together, is silhouetted against a sky fast growing pale and luminous. Left and right of it are similar groups, with intervals of a mile, or more, between. They are the outposts. Farther away still, as the light grows stronger you see occasional black specks of sentries sitting on ant-heaps, or moving slowly backward and forward—cold, hungry, miserable—who, the outermost line between Empire and Republics, have spent the night on the alert, so that the Division might sleep. Away on the right of your own brigade is another swarm of horses and waggons and guns, apparently grouped together haphazard and without any definite order. It is the other Brigade, all duly ordered in its regiments and squadrons and troops, but, in the distance, looking like a mob who have wandered together in the night and off-saddled promiscuously.

The world seems very still, and lifeless, and cold. As the day becomes more and more daylike, the long dry grass shines white with frost, and the huddled heaps of blankets are grey and stiff with it. It is on your overcoat, and little showers of it fall upon your boots drily, as you move through the grass.

Suddenly a hoarse voice raps out an order—there is no trumpeting at reveille on the march. The voice seems to have no effect. Again, and angrily, it rings out. It is a great and important voice—that of the regimental Sergeant-Major. Single figures flit about the lines, from heap to heap. More voices join in.

The heaps on the ground stir, and roll, and are convulsed by spasmodic internal movements. Strange figures in woollen nightcaps emerge from them slowly, and, one by one casting off their coverings, sit up, blinking and sleepy-eyed. They rise to their feet, fully dressed, and stretch themselves. A hasty shake and the buckling on of spurs is the only toilet. A sergeant comes striding down his troop, inquiring sarcastically whether the remaining heaps of blankets would like cups of tea brought to them. Corporals move about kicking up the sluggards. Slowly and stiffly man after man staggers, half-awake, to his horse, and commences to rub him down with more or less energy. Blankets are folded, white and wet still, and put on the horses' backs to serve as saddle-cloths. Then the bare saddles are girthed on, carbines stuck into 'buckets, ' and swords slipped into their 'frogs'. Where the heaps lay are only left the scanty domestic utensils—men's tins and meat cans—haversacks and bandoilers. The gun teams are being harnessed over in the Artillery lines. Nose-bags hang to the horses' heads—a quarter filled by two handfuls of oats.

Some one from the fires shouts "Coffee up! " and away go the corporals from each troop to carry over the steaming 'dixies'. There is a 'tinny' clatter, as the dregs and leaves of last night's tea are knocked out of the mess-tin lids against boots and picket-pegs, and little knots of cloaked figures swarm round the 'dixie' allotted to each troop, every one anxious lest he should miss his rightful proportion, which is barely half a pint. The great thing is to be in time when anything in the shape of rations is being doled out. In the English regiments each man puts his mess-tin on the ground. When all who have to share are present, the corporal fills each receptacle up evenly, and, if anything remains over distributes it in another round, no one venturing to touch his tin until all are served and the 'dixie' empty. This ensures 'a fair show' and no favour. But amongst the less well-regulated Australians it was usually a rush and a pushing in. It was impossible, always, for the distributor to remember each man whom he had served, and not a difficult thing for any one to 'come the double attack, ' but such meanness was rare, public opinion being too strong upon the point. One never knew when the exigencies of service might not render it impossible to be in the first rush, and it was accordingly self-protection, and not an altruistic feeling, that caused 'coming the double' to be sternly discountenanced by all and sundry.

You drink your apology for coffee while it is hot. Heat is its only virtue. Tasteless, almost sugarless, weak—it can rarely be regarded as a stimulant, never as likely to affect one's nerves—and consequently one's shooting. But 'something hot' before you start your march is as salvation, even though it be only hot water. Occasionally it is the only breakfast you have. If you are well looked after by your Quarter-master, however, there is generally a biscuit and some 'bully-beef'. Whatever it may be that you have, you eat it as you move about, between the packing of your wallets and the rolling of your overcoat. It does not do to be in un-ready when the 'prepare to mount' comes. The army biscuit is a thing not to be negotiated hastily, or approached flippantly. Eaten in its primitive hardness, without any soaking overnight in water, at least half an hour is occupied in the mastication of one biscuit. It is hard, tasteless, and nutritious—so nutritious that a man may at least keep body and soul together on one per diem, provided there be a bit of pumpkin, or a cob of mealies, to eke it out.

By the time you have broken your fast, you have put on and attached to your horse all the immense burden which that unfortunate quadruped is required to carry on active service. The wallets attached to either side of the pommel of the saddle are stuffed tight with your towel, minor effects, spare shirt (if you have one) and one hundred and fifty rounds of ammunition. Over them is strapped the rolled overcoat—wallets and coat together making up a weight well calculated to give the horse a sore wither. Underneath the saddle, as mentioned above, is the rider's sleeping blanket. Strapped to the cantle is the 'rear-pack, ' which may consist of anything from a rolled and empty waterproof sheet to a bundle of firewood. Attached to the rear-pack is usually an oat-sack containing from ten to fifteen, or even twenty pounds of grain—on the 'off' side hangs a heavy carbine in its leathern 'bucket'; on the 'near, ' a sword, useless except for potato-digging, and unnecessarily heavy by reason of its steel scabbard. From this side of the saddle also depends the feed-bag with the day's ration for the horse in it.

Wallets and overcoat on the wither, yourself in the middle of the horse's back, rear-pack, oat-sack, sword, carbine, feed-bag behind— little wonder is it that we fight indecisive rear-guard actions, that the sword is never used save as a tent-pole or a spade, that Steyn and Kruger are able to escape from Poplar Grove, although thousands of mounted men threaten their line of retreat to Bloemfontein. But the Red Book—the same Red Book whose teachings are of volleys fired standing up—has laid down the law, and so it is the law.

One cannot but pause here to consider this matter of the cavalryman's kit, since it has seemed to be responsible for so much ill success in the catching of commandos, in the cutting-off of the retreat of Boer armies, and in the raiding of the enemy's communications.

If you catch a Boer scout or vedette, you will wonder how he lives— he has so little of what seems to be regarded as the very necessaries of existence in our own lines. There are no wallets on his saddle, there is no heavy overcoat strapped across his pony's back. There is no rear-pack, or, as perhaps it might be more correctly named, 'loin-compress, ' to hinder the pony's action. There is no feed-bag to drag the saddle over to one side, so that it may press unevenly on his back. There is seldom anything but a bare saddle, without breast-plate or crupper, and a thin blanket beneath it. Sometimes a light mackintosh is strapped in front, with a little roll of biltong in a greasy rag. That is almost all. It is a matter of thirty seconds with him to saddle-up. He carries a bandolier, sometimes two, filled with the handy Mauser cartridge clips, over his shoulders. His rifle is slung across his back. His coat pockets contain a reserve supply of ammunition. And there you have the complete fighting man, from the Boer point of view. But of course he is grossly ignorant. If he only knew what was good for him, he too would resemble a Christmas tree, his movements would be slow and stately, his fat pony would be as like a hat-rack as ours became. He has not enjoyed the advantages conferred by a study of Red Books.

"I, " said the British troop horse (according to the Bloemfontein Friend), "I carry the most complete kit in the world. My master can make himself comfortable, even in your inhospitable veldt, with the kit I carry. "

"Yes, " replied the Boer pony, "but I can carry my master out of the way of yours. "

And yet, if you think about it, there is nothing in the equipment of a cavalry soldier on active service which may very well be dispensed with. He must have his overcoat. He must have his horse-feed. He must have his arms, and his feed-bag, and his blanket, and his ammunition. Most of the weighty things he carries are essential to his health or his arm of the service. They must all be somewhere within his reach. Cold or exposure would put him 'out of action' in a very short time, if he had no protection against wet or frosty nights. There must be occasional 'hard' feed to keep his horse fit for any work at all, and he must be able to get at his belongings easily when he bivouacs.

How is he to carry his necessaries along with him so that they are always easily within his reach, and at the same time 'travel light'? Waggons lag behind; Scotch carts get stuck in drifts. Even the ubiquitous Cape cart cannot always go over the same kind of country that he sometimes has to negotiate. There is one answer, one suggestion, which is not original perhaps, but which seems to be the only answer or suggestion which may adequately meet the want. And that is, Pack-horse.

Pack-horses, or light spring-carts—and the pack-horse has the virtue of greater mobility to turn the scale in his favour.

It is a fair estimate, and well within the mark, to assume that one pack-horse could carry the more urgently required effects of four men—that is to say, one weight-carrier to each section. Not all the rations, and horse-feed, and other things which the man may require on a march of many weeks, but the things which he cannot do without at night, and hardly needs in the day-time, and which are only a hindrance to his marching and fighting ability. There would be then, instead of four, five horses in each section—four to carry men, and one to carry baggage. When cavalry are dismounted for skirmishing, one man of every four—the horse-holder, or number three—is out of action. It is not very much more difficult to look after five horses than four. In work where there is a probability of being under fire, such as scouting or reconnoitring, the pack-leader might be left behind. There would be fewer men in the line of scouts, but the men who were there would be lighter, able to travel farther and faster with their reduced equipment than they are at present, and possessed of considerably more 'dash'—the great essential of a successful scout. Overcoat, waterproof sheet, cooking pots, anything beside the bare day's rations and cartridges—all that is not absolutely of use to the fighting man—might go on the pack-horse. And then the trooper, with an almost stripped saddle and riding as light as may be, would have some chance of catching his enemy and compelling him to fight. As it is now, he has very little.

So you mount your feeble steed, already weighed down by a load as great as yourself, and lurch along to where your troop is forming up in its squadron and regiment beside other squadrons and regiments. The advance guard has clattered out, and the outposts are drawing in to await the column. Other regiments form up to your left or right; the guns rumble up to their position near the lead. Carts and waggons begin to move up also into some sort of column formation. The bivouac-ground is deserted save by the inevitable laggards or men with sick horses who must follow slowly. Nearly every one is smoking. Troops are 'told off'—everything is ready for the march to begin. In the shadows before sunrise the dirty, travel-stained khaki figures seem dingier than ever. Dingy and dirty, but very fit and workmanlike. You sit and shiver, and wonder why the movement does not begin.

A little stout man on a good horse, followed by a group of red-collared staff officers, rides slowly through the ranks and up to the front, eyeing the troops. You sit up straight, and take your pipe out of your mouth. That little stout man is your father, and your mother, and your best friend just now, and he alone—may-be also one or two of the trim staff—has any idea as to what the day is going to bring forth. In an hour or two you may be dead, or a prisoner, or wounded, or wondering whether the next shell is going to land under your horse. You don't know what is going to happen, and use has made you careless. You are merely the pawn which that cheerful little man moves in the big game, and he, in his turn, is moved by a little slim man. It doesn't much matter what the day brings. You have confidence in French. He never goes wrong or makes a fool of you.

Now you are off—the horses' legs swish-swishing through the long grass; the mess-tins rattling against the carbine-butts; bits jingling musically; the bright sun just peeping over the edge of the world on your right hand; white puffs of tobacco smoke drifting up into the clear air. The veldt is turning to burnished gold. Your bridle-hand is frozen.

All round is laughter, and chaff, and quiet talk. Curious scraps of conversation drift to you as you ride along.

"... Fifty miles to the Vaal. Bill's got a map, an' we measured it. They're goin' ter make a stand there. Lord Roberts's over there— along th' railway. Some one else t'other side o' him. Goin' ter be a heavy scrap along the river... had a dog that useter walk along a top-rail fence. One day, out a must'rin'... so I sez to the Dutch woman, wot the 'ell d'yer wanter keep on fightin', an' actin' th' goat like this for; y' know dam well yer licked, I sez, an' she sez 'Voetsak'... got two cow-guns with 'em... went ter Gunnedah races, an' got took down... any bacca?... wonder wot'll win the Melbourne Cup. Now, I reckon... Hole!... That's Johnny French up there—him on th' chestnut. Clever little bloke, ain't 'e?... got two pounds of mealie-meal, an' some coffee, an' half a dozen bundles of hay. No sugar... presently I begins ter twig wot they was at. So I sings out to Jimmy, 'Come on!' an' we sails inter them with chairs an' bottles, an' gets outside inter th' yard. Pretty willin' go it was too... Hole!... look out—y'r' jammin' me int' him, keep over... better General than Wellington, so he is... hope th' swine gets a bullet next time. Ain't fit ter lead ducks, let alone... Hole!"—and so forth.

Strange lies are bandied about as to the doings of Buller. He has occupied Johannesburg—no, Harrismith. Mafeking has fallen. Steyn is dead. De Wet wants to surrender, if they'll promise not to send him to St. Helena. The probability of getting full rations soon is discussed, and negatived. The ways of officers are criticised.

The sun mounts higher and higher, and your hands and toes begin to thaw. The little black dots of scouts who occasionally come into view on the far sky-lines are more distinct. Odd men walk along, leading their horses after them, to keep warm.

On, through the bright morning hours, you ride—past white-walled farmhouses, down long, gentle slopes clothed with deep grasses, by Kaffir kraals whose dusky inhabitants gape with wonder at the numbers of the rooineks, and where the little pot-bellied niggers gaze out, goggle-eyed and fearful, from behind their ample mothers. Sometimes the column narrows into a long procession to cross a deep spruit, and forms up again slowly into 'mass' upon the other side.

Barbed-wire fences are encountered. The cry goes up, "Wire-cutters to the front! " and two or three men from each squadron race on ahead, and sever the wires with their clippers, pulling them aside that the Brigade may pass. A thankless job wirecutting, especially when the bullets are flying. Sometimes the fences have stone posts — slabs of a slaty sandstone which the natives quarry from the hills, and supply to the farmers at sixpence apiece. Fire-proof fences these, and fairly lasting, one would think. Here and there a post is broken down. Struck by lightning, people who know the country will tell you.

A long kopje looms up over the horizon. You are riding towards it for hours. Distance is strangely foreshortened in this clear atmosphere. A few miles from it the column halts. The men are dismounted, and lie down beside their horses. The scouts are riding on ahead to 'draw fire'. You pillow your head upon your helmet and go to sleep, whilst your horse crops the grass about you, and barely refrains from trampling on your prostrate form. A sudden scramble awakes you. Everybody is mounting again.

The kopje is unoccupied, and you ride on past it. The farmhouse under its shoulder flies five white flags. A Boer woman comes out and stares at you stolidly. If the Provost-Marshal and his men do not seem to be looking, you slip away from your troop, and, while your messmate haggles with the woman at the doorway over the price of eggs or mealie-meal, you endeavour to steal a fowl or a duck — that is to say, you seek to 'commandeer' them. Convenient word 'commandeer'. If you are fortunate, you put the broken-necked bird in your feed-bag, and it represents five pounds of oats, and is not too inconveniently in evidence.

At noon you halt once more, and eat some biscuits and anything else that you may happen to have, and take a drink from your water-bottle, and sleep again on the ground for half an hour or more.

So all day, the swarm of men and horses, guns and waggons, rolls across the veldt — a wide-spreading oncoming — like a plague of locusts. On the whole, it is pleasant, and enjoyable, and lazy. Sitting loose in the saddle, you smoke and yarn, and speculate as to where you are and what you are going to do, and how long it will be before you are in Pretoria. You have made up your mind that Pretoria is to end it all. You are going home then—back to the station, or the office, or the store, and the warm welcome you know is waiting. Perhaps it will be a trip to England, where you will be fêted and made much of, and generally given a good time. It is days and days since you heard a rifle fired; weeks and weeks, perhaps, since a gun boomed out over the plains. All the Boers have fled to the Vaal—probably across it, without stopping, to Johannesburg and Pretoria. There will be a siege, possibly, for a month. You will sit upon a hill and watch the shelling. The lyddite will soon bring them to their senses, once they are fairly bottled up in a town, with the bricks and stones tumbling about their ears. It is all very simple and straightforward now. You will be back in time for shearing.

Another kopje rises up ahead. Closer and closer you get to it, though it is still miles away. A very long one this time—camel-backed, and with little foot-hills and clumps of 'wacht-een-beetje' bush in front of it. A single horseman comes galloping back from where the scouts are, and stops at the staff. Again the Division halts, and sits down and wonders. Ten minutes, and you see the Colonel talking to your particular squadron leader. They argue, and point, and look through glasses, and consult maps. Finally the Major nods, rolls his map up, picks up his loose reins, says something sharply that is only audible in the leading troop, and you suddenly mount, and find yourself riding out from the middle of the Brigade towards the blue kopje in the distance. Friendly souls advise you not to stay too long—not to get excited. "Meet y' in Pretoria if y' don't come back to-night, " calls out a humorous acquaintance.

"We're off to stir up th' muck agin, " remarks your right-hand man philosophically.

CHAPTER IV - THE KOPJE

THE Brigade was halted close beside a white farmhouse. There had been slaughter and rapine in the poultry-yard; bundles of hay had been looted from the forage-loft. We left them sitting on the ground beside their horses. The feed-bags with the scanty oats had been hung on the drooping heads, and all, save ourselves and the squadron of which our diminished two troops formed part, were resting, and seemed likely to rest for some hours. While they rested we were to ride out and 'feel' that long, blue kopje.

Every one knew what the 'business' was from long experience. The kopje looked peaceful and quiet in the warm afternoon sunlight. Unless one had seen it all before, and had previous knowledge of lovely landscapes that spat bullets from apparently nowhere in particular, one would hardly have expected that an hour or two would bring one within touch of sudden death. The first time it had been a riding forth without reason, a light-hearted excursion into the debatable lands—an astonished feeling of resentment that so harmless and smiling a prospect should merely be a mask hiding an unknown foe. Frequently afterwards the objective had been a mystery. Troop leaders may have known what they were required to find out, and how they were going to set about it, and where the enemy was supposed to be 'lying low, ' but the trooper seldom had any definite notion as to what was to be done, or what was expected of him. There may have been Mauser-fire, or there may have been shell-fire to be drawn. He was not consulted in the matter. He was merely sent out as a bait for bullets. Often recurring experience of the kind of thing in question had made it familiar. Familiarity had almost bred contempt. If bullets pass closely by, without hitting you, on nine separate occasions, you feel tolerably certain that you will come off scatheless on the tenth.

So you go out, with no serious apprehension as to whether you will return to camp at night. Sometimes, to be sure, you don't—but the chance is so small as to be barely worth consideration. Usually, you are not even curious as to what the work in hand may be. It is vaguely probable that it will consist of the well-known 'drawing fire, ' but you don't know for certain, and after a while you don't care overmuch.

To-day, however, there is no doubt. The wide, yellow veldt sweeps away to the horizon—East, West and South unbrokenly. It is only to the North that the long kopje mars the even symmetry of the sky-line. You are riding towards it. You are well extended from your neighbour. A few advanced scouts are in front. You know what to expect.

The plains are not quite level. Gentle slopes run down, for a mile or more, into shallow spruits and rain-cut dongas. The waving grass is dry, and has lost its first freshness by reason of the frosts. Up from the further side of each donga the ground rises slowly to another low crest. No ridge is higher than its fellow; no depression deeper than the one before it. The air is clear and bright, but the distant landscape is half-veiled by a gauzy, purple haze, just dense enough to render indistinct horses and men moving about over two thousand yards away. You might see them, but they would not be sharply defined targets.

Here and there on the slopes are the humpy, mud-coloured kraals of the Kaffirs—'Gunyahs' Tommy Cornstalk calls them. They are quaint structures, primitive and simple. In shape they are like hollow globes divided into two halves at the equators, and the halves planted, pole skyward, on the ground. Sometimes they are plastered with mud—a kind of 'wattle and daub'—sometimes thatched with grass. A tiny arched hole in the side, through which it is necessary to crawl in order to enter, is the only opening. There is no provision for light or ventilation. Fires, apparently, are made outside. Round the diminutive doorway there is usually a little wicket fence constructed of sticks from the scant bushes of the kopjes, or of mealie-stalks lashed together—the top of the palisading uncut and ragged. In occasional more pretentious establishments the fence surrounds the whole hut. Three-legged cooking pots and gourds are heaped by the doorway inside. Fowls run in and out of the enclosure. The ground all about is trampled hard, and seems to be kept clean and well swept.

Close beside the man-kraals are the cattle-kraals—low-walled, square or oblong yards built of the loose, undressed, unmortared stones that litter the veldt. Wonderfully well-built and 'plumb' are these stone-age stock-yards—laborious of construction probably, but, without doubt, lamb-proof and dog-proof. A single entrance at one end, closed by rails, serves to admit the stock.

About the dwellings, as you pass by, are grouped the dusky family—the men-kind ranging from bent and white-headed veterans, who might have beheld the Great Trek or fought the Voortrekkers, to tiny, podgy fellows just able to walk abroad naked and unashamed; and the women from withered hags, toothless and wrinkled, down to bright-eyed little maidens of few summers. In his prime, the Kaffir is a fine man—deep-chested, sturdy-haunched, light-hearted—and the women, broad-hipped, deep-bosomed, cavern-mouthed and flat-faced, but not altogether unpleasing in appearance. The fat, barrel-bodied children goggle with astonishment and run as you ride by. No bad country this, where the babies are so fat and the mothers so strong and comely—where the mealie crops are sown, and come up and flourish, in fields that have been but barely scratched by way of cultivation.

Kaffir kraals are not bad places to drop into when your haversack is empty and your wallets innocent of sustenance. That is to say, there is generally something to be had—if a commando has not passed that way in retreat, or if there be no Mounted Infantry ponies hanging to the cornstalk fence, with big wooden, leather-covered stirrups, and overcoats tied carelessly to the back of the black saddle with string or oxhide that hang loose over the horses' flanks. If you see that kind of pony, with that kind of stirrup, and that method of rolling a cloak, you will know that the Canadians are within—and to go a-foraging where the Canadians are doing likewise, or may have been, argues bad judgment and an ill-balanced brain.

War is not a nice business, and an empty stomach has no conscience. Orlando's method of demanding food from the Duke in the Forest of Arden was rude and brusque, and not to be extenuated—but there were points about it. If you have had nothing to eat since last night, and see no prospect of anything to-night, few scruples will prevent you from obtaining it in the most expeditious manner possible—if it is to be obtained. You know also that, if you do not take it, some one else will. So you ride up to your kraal. "Got any mealie, Johnny? " to the head of the household.

"Nie mealie, baas. "

"Any eggs? " (If he doesn't understand, you point to the fowls, and make gestures.) "Nie, baas. "

"Melk? "

"Nie melk, baas. "

You draw your carbine from its bucket, insert a cartridge in the breech, and rest it across your legs. The movement is not lost on the head of the household. "Any mealie now, Johnny? "

"Ja, baas. "

"Any eggs? "

"Ja, baas! "

"Any melk? "

"Ja, baas! Ja! ja! ja! "

And mealies, and milk, and eggs are forthcoming from the kraal, with perhaps a fowl thrown in as a voluntary peace-offering. If you have any money, you give him some. If you have none, you ride away, and feel sorry for the Kaffirs, and moralise inwardly on the iniquity of war and its usages. It is brutal, but imperative.

"Sanguinary rough, " says Tommy Cornstalk, "to take the poor devils' tucker. But I was hungry. " And that explains it. One must live, even at the expense of others. It is simply the law of self-preservation stripped of the clothing worn by it in civilisation. You do the same thing every day at home, only you don't notice it.

The blue kopje draws nearer. Only a mile or two now. There will be shooting and riding soon. You wonder whether that 'off' fore-shoe will bring you to grief. You are trotting most of the time—that wretched English trot which helps the 'Tommies' to give their horses sore backs, and which is the only pace these London cab horses seem to know. They were given to you as remounts at Bloemfontein, after the race thither and sundry ridings round Thaba N'chu had used up the last of the good Australians you shipped at Woolloomooloo a few months back. You feel that you want a bell or a whistle, in order to get the best work out of your over-burdened, underfed mount.

By this time you are the fourth part of a 'left flanking patrol'. The main body of the reconnoitring squadron rides some distance to the rear of a widely extended line of scouts. You are level with the squadron, but half a mile further out to the left than the last of the scouts. It is your business to prevent a possibly lurking enemy from 'nippin' in behind, ' or 'attacking sideways on'—as it has variously been put. The squadron is a little cluster of horsemen, extended also, but not too widely to render them an unattractive target for artillery. They will draw the shell-fire, if there be any to be had. The scouts will count the Mausers.

A mealie field has to be ridden through. There are possibilities about mealie fields. The stalks are high enough in parts almost to hide a man on horseback. They may shelter a few hidden sharpshooters, or they may contain a commando. You open out wider as you enter, and ride through the rustling ears and leaves with your loaded rifle ready in your hand.

There is no one there. Just on the further edge is one of those circular, circus-ring threshing grounds, where the women beat out the Kaffir corn—a species of millet with little round seeds tufting together at its top, from which, when ground between stones, they make a coarse bread. To-day there are two fat 'gins' and a girl, so busily engaged in bagging the winnowed seed that you burst upon them suddenly from amid the mealie crop—so suddenly that the eldest and stoutest of the three comes near to having a fit, and can only gasp and stare at you in an agonised, helpless way. The girl, shapely and wellmade, comes forward laughing. But she cannot speak English.

"Where Boers? " you inquire.

"Boos! " she says, catching at the word; "Boos? "

"Ja, Boos! where you think it that pheller him go? " you reply, dropping unconsciously into Australese. But she can only shake her head and smilingly bare a gleaming set of perfect teeth. After much gesture, you are not quite certain whether she means to imply that the veldt ahead is swarming with Boers, or that they have all trekked to an indefinite distance, hurriedly and wholesale.

Kaffir information is seldom to be depended upon when you are scouting. Few people other than the Kaffir will probably assent so readily to any interrogative address, if it be that he thinks that a reply in the affirmative will be acceptable to the questioner. Similarly, if he suppose that 'no' will gratify, he will say no. He is quite impartial. He will give you any information you please. Whether it be correct matters not to him, so long as it satisfies you.

"There are horses in that kraal, aren't there, Johnny? "

"Ja, baas. "

"You've never seen a horse in your life, have you, Johnny? "

"No, baas. "

When in doubt he says "Ja".

"Which would you sooner do or play cricket, Johnny? "

"Ja, baas. "

One refers, of course, to the Kaffir whose only alien tongue is Dutch. He is a guileless liar, and generally doesn't know when he is lying and when he is speaking the truth. At any rate, it is the safest course, when your life may depend upon it, never to accept information from a Kaffir as being wholly reliable. You may usually only arrive at an approximation to the truth by carefully comparing the lies, and putting two and two together from the whole mass of fiction.

Half a mile beyond the mealie field and about halfway up the opposite gentle slope, was a collection of mud huts. The main body had halted temporarily, so it seemed to the 'left flanking patrol' an excellent opportunity for supplementing a deplenished larder. A man remained on his horse a hundred and fifty yards out beyond the kraal, and the rest cautiously approached the enclosure. It might have been a trap—but wasn't.

At the door was the oldest woman in the world—the oldest woman who had ever lived in the world. Shrivelled to what might have been half her size in youth; bent, until her head was almost lower than her hips; almost without sight or hearing; long skinny breasts depending loosely and hideously from her shrunken chest; spindleshanked, nearly naked, unintelligent—she was not unlike Gagool of King Solomon's Mines. Crouched in the sun when we rode up, she seemed hardly to notice us, and remained squatting in the same place until we went away. It seemed impossible that there could have been an older man or woman in existence.

"One hundred and fifty, " said the corporal, "if she's a day! "—and indeed she looked it. A white-headed 'Uncle Ned, ' who was probably her grandson, strolled about near her. Little niggers swarmed all round.

This family seemed particularly impressed by our appearance— which was probably picturesque, if not clean. Almost ere we could requisition anything, a bowl of eggs was brought, and a gourd full of sweet goat's milk, and, by signs and jabbering, they tendered the fullest hospitality they had. No need this time for 'moral suasion,' in the form of rifle loading!

It is perhaps uncharitable to say so, but in the light of subsequent events their hospitality can hardly seem to have been anything but a lure—an encouragement to ride on carelessly, and to assume that there were no Boers in the neighbourhood by reason of the Kaffirs' friendliness. Bullets came from that kraal later in the day, as the reconnoitring party retired. But the eggs were good, and we sucked them.

The watcher without hailed us: —

"Come on, you fellows. The push's going on. Buck up! Wot yer got?"

So we went on up the rise. Half a mile and the crest was reached. Keeping step with the main body, we again halted, and looked out over the wide rolling veldt. The haze was deeper and more blue now, and the scouts were nearing the long kopje.

From the crest where we were the ground sloped away in a series of undulations down to a level plain. From the foot of the slope—which was scarcely noticeable, and only so because the curtain of haze seemed to begin there—the plain reached flat and far and unbroken, past the kopje we were interested in, to a distant range of indigo hills. And in the plain manoeuvred two squadrons of cavalry, moving parallel to and in the same direction as ourselves.

Whom could they be? We sat and watched them from our saddles, whilst our own squadron, three-quarters of a mile to the right, remained stationary.

Now there should have been no British troops so close up on our left. The First Cavalry Brigade we had come from. To the right of it was the Fourth. Hutton's Mounted Infantry was behind. It was just possible, though very improbable, that a couple of companies of

Hutton's men had come up on our left, in order to reconnoitre the country further to the west. Improbable, because they could hardly have reached there in the time. However, as it is usual to send out reconnoitring parties without giving each individual an intelligent insight into the 'lay of the land, ' and the whereabouts of other divisions, it still remained possible. That they were using our troop formation, and riding in fairly regular order—with advanced scouts out in front—lent colour to the supposition that they were British and not Boer. That they were in a position whither one was almost certain no British troops could have come without our having discovered them earlier in the afternoon seemed to point to the fact that they were Boer and not British.

We sat undecided. Up ahead, the scouts were halted—tiny specks of men and horses in the haze—apparently right under the long kopje, really half a mile from it. How were we to make sure of the newcomers on our left? The strange squadrons had halted likewise by this time. Two or three leaders seemed to be riding amongst the ranks. We knew not what to make of them. Oh, for the field-glasses which we should have carried rather than the useless swords. Presently some twenty detached themselves from the main body and came riding towards us. More mysterious still! Nearer and nearer they came. A slight depression hid them from us.

Far away, and faintly from the long kopje, came the quick double report of a Mauser—ping-pong. Then again rapidly, ping-pong, ping-pong, ping-ping, pongpong—p-r-r-r-r-p—the scouts had drawn their fire. Crack-crack, crack-crack-cr-r-rr-r-r-ack—cr-r-r-r-r-r-ack—the cordite answered, which was contrary to wont. The scouts were retiring slowly, covering their retreat with rifle-fire. Sometimes it died away to a single ping-pong or crack; then again it ripped and rolled across the veldt in a stronger medley of sound. We sat watching our uncertain neighbours on the left. Their main body had turned as the scouts turned, and were edging in towards our rear.

Out of the depression where the twenty had disappeared, eight hundred yards away, came riding a single big man on a white pony. No sign was there of the twenty who had started with him.

Said the corporal: "That settles it. They're British, and they're sending across to find out who the devil we are. Come on! We'll go and meet him! " So we rode slowly over.

The distance from the hollow became less than six hundred.

"Hadn't I better get down and cover the bloke? " some one queried of the corporal. "He might be a Bore after all. Best not give him any show. "

"Well, I don't know, " said the corporal, "I— —"

Phutt-bang! phutt-bang! (the Mauser only sounds double in the distance) phutphut-phut-bang-bang-bang! —bullets came singing and spitting past our ears and made little red spirits of dust beyond our horses on the ground. Phut-phut-phut-t-t-tt-bang-bang-bang-b-r-r-r-r-ump!

"Oh, Lord! " said the corporal, "time we left. What a sell! Come on! Files about. They're trying to cut us off! "

Back we went at a hand-gallop, the little spirts of dust and the phut-phut-phut of the singing nickel growing less frequent and close as the distance lessened between ourselves and the main body. The scouts were nearly back to it also now, riding slowly, apparently out of range of the long, blue, innocent-looking kopje. No one had been hit. A bullet intended for the 'left flanking patrol' had sailed merrily overhead, and, almost spent, dropped into the belly of a horse with the main body. The horse lived and worked for a week.

That is the inexplicable thing about 'drawing fire'—how so little damage is done. All the advantages would seem to lie with the hidden rifleman whose fire is to be 'drawn'. The horseman is an enlarging target as he approaches. The man in the rocks may choose the position for shooting which he fancies best, may select his favourite range, may pick his man—but he seldom hits him.

Once, a troop consisting of four-and-twenty men and two officers went forth to investigate a mine superstructure and a 'tailing-heap, ' close by Roodepoort on the Rand. There were from one hundred to one hundred and fifty Boers in a deep ditch—a 'surface drive' it would be in Australia—which lay just before the buildings. Thirty feet in front of the ditch stretched a barbed-wire fence, and the ditch was not visible until the fence was reached. The troop came to the fence, and drew a paralysing volley. They wheeled and raced. For several hundred yards, before the slope of the ground hid them from sight, they were under the rapid Mauser magazine-fire. There were bullets through helmets, haversacks, clothing, saddlery and two horses—but that was all!

Yet, if you think of it, the first shot is the only one that may be effective. And the marksman generally makes too sure—just as you are liable to miss a kangaroo at twenty feet if you don't take the usual pains over aligning the sights. And when once the horseman has turned, and is increasing the range with every second, he is the poorest target possible. You may pump lead at him, but you don't hit him. You will probably forget to adjust your back-sight as he alters the range from five to seven hundred yards.

Another explanation of the often very bad shooting of the Boer is that the Mauser—a comparatively new weapon to him—is marked in metres, whereas he has learned to shoot in yards with the old Martini or the American-pattern rifles. But that is as may be.

The squadron was trotting back by this time to where it had parted from the Brigade—scouts as a rear-guard. Away back, little dots were sliding out of the long kopje and slithering over the veldt in pursuit. A properly carried out reconnaissance entails something of the distasteful upon the men who carry it out. It is unpleasant, and a trifle humiliating, to be chased—more natural to stand and fight. But it is the proper game—to run when you have drawn the enemy's fire. You are not there to fight him. You are to find him out, and go back for your big brother to wallop him.

The 'left flanking patrol' of the advance had become the 'right flanking patrol' of the retirement, but the retirement was slightly oblique, and half a mile further east than the line of advance.

Opposite the kraal where Gagool lived more bullets came spitting by. From near the mealie field another shower. Beyond the mealie field, the troop leader sent the writer with one man on a pleasant mission. We were to ride out to the right, six hundred yards, and see whether there was any donga or spruit where the enemy might be concealed in order to rake the main body as it passed by. "Goodbye, " said the troop humorously, "see you on the Day of Judgment! " It seemed likely.

Out six hundred yards there were no bullets. Out fifty more and the air above our heads hummed with them. But they came from a cluster of galvanised iron huts nearly a thousand yards away.

The Division was riding up to meet us—a long line of horses and khaki. Bang! went a Horse Artillery gun, and the shell 'whooshled' over our heads to check the advancing Boers. Pom-pom-pom! and the little one-pounders of the Vickers-Maxim scurried away on the same mission. A few hundred New Zealanders from Hutton's Brigade rode out in open order and passed through us.

The Division swung round to the right. Bang! bang! —a couple more guns. A premature shell-burst spattered the veldt with shrapnel just in front of the Maorilanders. We joined the regiment.

Beyond doubt it had been proved that the long kopje contained Boers—'Quod erat demonstrandum'!

The Division moved along down a shallow depression towards a great dam. We were to bivouac. The fight, if there was one, would come off next day. From ahead came the rip-rip-rip! of the New Zealanders' rifles. The Mauser bullets were splashing up the dust as they fell spent three hundred yards from us. We came to our camping-ground. The fire died away with the dusk.

There had been an incident which we learnt of only that evening. As the scouts were advancing, the horse of a shoeing-smith of the 'Greys' had stumbled in an ant-bear hole. The rider's leg was broken, and his mate stayed with him. When we retired they had been far off our line of retreat, and had been forgotten. The friend of the injured man, under a hail of bullets from the on-coming Boers, had galloped back with the led horse. Up came the Boer Commandant to where the helpless smith lay.

"What? badly hurt, old man? Sorry; hard luck! Have a drink of water. Wish I had whisky to offer you! "—and he passed on, being in a hurry to get in another shot at the 'verdomde rooineks'.

CHAPTER V - THE OUTPOST

If you have ridden all day through the Bush with the thermometer at one hundred and five degrees Fahrenheit in the shade, you are naturally pleased at sundown when you dimly realise that here at last is rest, and a temporary cessation of the overpowering attentions of the flies. You swing to the ground, glad to stretch your cramped limbs, slip the saddle from the hack, and the pack-saddle from the packhorse—tumbling them anyhow on the grass—and proceed to hobble the horses. You collect little sticks, and make a fire; spread out your blankets, and watch the quart boil; put in the tea, and thank God that, for eight or nine hours the small worries of life on the road will not beset you. You take your hat off, and feel at peace with all men.

To you enter a confounded hairy man. In language less polite than to the point he intimates that you have camped in his cultivation paddock; that your parentage is doubtful, and your bringing-up disastrous; that he has never in his life beheld a person so divinely dowered with impudence as yourself; and that he will not feel obliged to you if you remove yourself and your belongings elsewhere. He will in no wise feel hurt if you decide to deny his paddock the benefit of your presence for the night, in fact he insists upon your doing so.

You point out to him that nothing remains of the finest wheat crop in the district save stubble, that the water-hole in his creek is the only water to be met with in many miles, that you are exceedingly fatigued, and that he is a d——d ill-grained swine. Which latter statement does not placate him, and you are obliged to go.

It is your own fault. When you jumped that dogleg fence you knew well that you ran the risk of subsequent ejection by a hairy man. Trespass was writ large in barbed-wire. It is no more than you might have expected. Nevertheless, it is the Dead Finish.

When you have ridden all day across the veldt, with the strength of your mount at one quarter horse-power, you are not sorry when the Adjutant demands 'markers' from your corps to align the position of your horse-lines in the camping-ground. You may have been scouting half the day. You may have been 'drawing fire, ' or fighting a wearisome and desultory rear-guard action. Your rations may have been in the raw, as uncooked meat and flour; and by reason of not having had sufficient halting space all day to prepare them for consumption, you may have gone hungry. You may have been looking forward to getting the burden of saddlery and kit off your weary beast, and giving him to eat what little of oats remains in your attenuated feed-bag. You may have been fortunate in the matter of loot, and have a fowl in your haversack, together with a few potatoes and a little mealie-meal in your wallets. The bandolier, with sixty cartridges, and water-bottle, and haversack will have been cramping your shoulders. You are looking forward to a good 'feed, ' and a subsequent pipe beside the fire you are going to kindle out of the fence-post you have carried in front of you for the last hour or more. And then the fine sleep you will have—the welcome, friendly forgetfulness—when you can dream that you are back again in a land of peace once more, where there are no homes wrecked, and you must go out of your way a little to stumble across misery and distress.

When you have found your lines, and driven in your picket-peg with the hilt of your sword, and unstrapped your overcoat and rear-pack, and taken off your saddle and 'dressed' it with the others in a line in front of the horses, under the direction of a pedantically accurate sergeant-major, you feel that here, at least, is peace, that for a few precious hours you will be left to yourself and the attendance upon your own very pressing personal needs.

To you enter an execrable hairy man. In brief but unanswerable terms he warns your troop for 'outpost'. As an afterthought, he enjoins upon you the necessity for 'looking slippery'. Your single swearword speaks volumes. You will roll your coat again; you will strap up your rear-pack; you will adjust the many-buckled saddlery; you will don the harness of water-bottle, and haversack, and bandolier once more. You will mount and ride again, and above all you will look forward joylessly to a night without food or fire, and an interrupted sleep. This again is the Dead Finish.

There are few colloquialisms more expressive of wearisome disgust, dissatisfaction and discontent than is 'Dead Finish'. It is almost synonymous with 'the Last Straw'.

The troop goes out. There are twelve men, a sergeant and a couple of corporals with a subaltern officer in charge. Everything is carried as on the march. The Adjutant will accompany your officer to point out to him the position you are to take up. It is almost dark. Behind, as you ride out over the veldt, glimmer the little fires of the bivouac, and the subdued hum is wafted to you of thousands of men busy with the preparation of their evening meal.

A simultaneous whinny from the lines tells you that the feed-bags are being put upon the horses. The metallic click-click-click of a picket-peg being driven in sounds faint and far away. Presently you rise over what is the skyline from the camp, and are alone in the night. Miles and miles ahead a single starlike gleam marks some far off Boer watch-fire. Out in the east, over the long kopje of the day's work, the sky is paling. There will be moonlight soon.

What a deuce of a distance we are going out to-night! It seems hours and hours since we saddled up disgustedly and left the lines—the luxurious lines, where there is food, and rest, and sleep. There will be an issue of bully-beef to-night, and we shall miss it. If the carts come up, it is rum night. We shall miss that also. D——n outpost! D——n everything! What is it all worth—this weary, worked out, unsatisfactory old war? Why not have stayed at home, and lived the old life unbrokenly? We would be sitting down to dinners and teas now—in clean shirts and more or less fine raiment. There would have been a good smoke, a game of billiards, a theatre, a dance, music, newspapers—and then, a warm bed with clean sheets on it. Think of it—clean sheets! Clean sheets and a full stomach—surely that is heaven!

Why couldn't England have 'bucked up' and fought her old war herself? We're not getting anything out of it. We're losing time, and money, and place. We have made ourselves liable to be spoken to as though we were serfs and not free Australians by any bumptious boy calling himself 'Second Lieutenant'. Second Lieutenant! Ye gods—by any 'bounder' of a sergeant-major, by any cocky corporal, by any new-chum wearer of the lance stripe. We have dug latrines, and buried mules, and made graves. We are crawling with vermin. We are tired, and stiff, and hungry, and we are going out 'on outpost'.

Why did we ever come? This isn't charging into battle. This isn't racing through a flying foe. This isn't getting the Victoria Cross. Where is all the 'pomp and circumstance of war'? Where are the bands and the martial music to play us into action? Where are the clouds of drifting smoke we've read about? Where's that 'thin red line, ' and all those gorgeous uniforms that used to make war picturesque, and romantic, and spectacular? Where's anything but dirt, and discomfort, and starvation, and nigger-driving? Who wants to participate in a shabby war like this?

Oh, you growling swine, Tommy Cornstalk! If you had been rejected, been sent home from Randwick because of your varicose vein or your hollow tooth; fallen off your horse in the riding test, or failed to hit the target when you were tried on the range—you know well what it would have meant. Can't you think of how you would have gone back to the station or the township, downcast and shame-faced? Don't you remember how lucky you thought you were when you marched down George Street to the 'trooper'? What about the hour or two when all the people were howling mad over you, when the girls you didn't know came and kissed you, when the effusive males who didn't go themselves handed you bottles of beer to quench the magnificent thirst you had cultivated betwixt the barracks and the boat? How did you feel then? Don't you really— deep down in your heart—consider that you are getting your reward?

Isn't it something to be marching, and fighting, and starving with these Englishmen? Supposing that they are the scum of England—if they are—isn't it something for a one-horse volunteer crowd like you to be a squadron of such a regiment as the one you are with—a regiment which was fighting before there was an Australia, a regiment which saw Waterloo and Balaclava? And another thing— isn't it something to have shown a regiment like that how to scout, how to take cover, how to ride, how to shoot; how, in short, to play this particular game as it should be played, and in the only way by which there is possibility of success? Isn't that something, you discontented dog?

Go—go out to your comfortless outpost. Have no supper. Make no fire. Just take your two hours' watch, and your four hours' sleep in your lousy blanket, and thank God that you are privileged to be here—yes, privileged—instead of reading about it in newspapers and books, and not knowing.

The position assigned to the outpost is just below the skyline of another ridge. One can hardly speak of these almost invisible elevations as 'ridges'. The plain, when you ride over it, seems nearly quite level, and viewed from afar it seems to be so also; but there are little watersheds in it which form the ridges and the valleys, and the dongas in the valleys. If you are on a crest, you see more land, and the horizon is farther off than when you are below it. It is not unlike a calm sea, with just a long swell humping it up into faintly visible hillsides of wave and trough—level as a whole, but not in detail. An outpost placed upon the summit of one of these 'waves' would be conspicuous against the sky to an enemy approaching from the front. Accordingly, it is usually stationed a hundred or two hundred yards below the crest, and sentries are placed out far enough to command a view of the country from which attack may be expected. When you have come to your allotted place in the ring of outposts you are 'numbered off' from the right.

"One, two and three—first relief; four, five and six—second relief; seven, eight and nine—third relief, " says the sergeant. That is to say, that the first three men will furnish the first round of sentries, who will do duty for two hours until relieved by the second group. Their places, in turn, will be taken by the third. Thus, the first sentries will have four hours in which to sleep before being called up again. Each corporal will take one of two of the remaining, and patrol between his own and the next post at three—or four—hourly intervals. The odd man will be kept as an emergency. He is liable to be called and sent out at any hour, but as a rule has a full night's sleep. His is the lightest 'duty' in the outpost, but may quite easily become the hardest, according to circumstances.

From a larger outpost, 'Cossack posts' are often sent out. A 'Cossack-post' consists of a N. C.O. and three men, who picket their horses a considerable distance from the main post, and provide one sentry at a time. They are usually placed in isolated positions, where it would be unwise to risk a larger body of men, or between two posts, when the distance separating them is greater than usual.

The two first sentries are stationed some two hundred yards out in front, and from two to four hundred yards apart. The third man of the relief watches over the horses, and is ready to rouse his sleeping comrades in case of an alarm. He carries a time-piece, if such a thing is available, and, five minutes before his two hours expire, calls the sergeant, who posts the next three men. Each of the corporals takes his man and rides out to find the right or left-hand post—a by no means easy task in this open veldt, where an absence of landmarks and similarity of country tax one's powers of 'bushcraft' to the utmost. After placing his sentries, and giving them the countersign, the officer in charge returns to his post with the sergeant. The sergeant's duties for the remainder of the night consist of 'marching' the reliefs every two hours. He is also responsible to the officer for the conduct of affairs, and the correct timing of the goings out of the 'reliefs' and 'patrols'.

The moon has risen over the dark hump of the long kopje. The worn out, still saddled horses cast weird shadows over the grass—one or two lying down, the others forlornly engaged in cropping so much of it around their pegs as the head-ropes will allow. The men have put on their overcoats—those excellent cavalry cloaks which are the best part of the equipment—and are busy unrolling waterproof sheets and in slipping their blankets from beneath the saddle. Strictly, the blankets should remain where they have been all day, but these nights are too cold to lie down without some means of warmth other than this cloak, and so the loss of them is risked by their owners. Should the post be rushed, or attacked, there would be no time to remove the saddles and replace the blankets beneath them, and they would have to be abandoned, unless carried away on their owners' arms. Fortunately, however, for the comfort of outposts, Boers do not often attack. When they do, there is usually no 'get away'.

The outpost is tired to-night, and does not talk much. There has been no tea, because it was too late to light fires. Nothing to eat, either, but a possible biscuit. Some one was to have come from the camp with bully-beef, but seems to have lost the way, or not to have started. So it is a far from hilarious outpost. A man is speaking in low tones on the subject of dealing with coloured races.

"W'en me brother Mick was in Mason's survey camp—doin' axeman—he come across a cove out near Walgett who had a black feller with him drovin'. This bloke useter bring cattle in from Queensland ter Muswellbrook. Went by the name o' Kale—K-a-l-e— rum name. Useter give th' nigger a quid a month and his rations. Good enough for a nigger, too.

"Ev'ry now 'n-then, th' nigger useter wanter be settled up with, an' Kale'd look at a book an' pretend to be squarin' up his account. 'Well, Jacky, ' Kale'd say, 'y' got a pound er terbacca on the fifteenth? '—'Yes, that right, ' Jacky'd say. 'Well, that's a pound y' got, an' a pound y' didn't get, ain't it? '—'Yes, alright, ' Jacky'd say. 'That's two pound, ain't it? ' Kale'd arst him. —'Yes, that right, ' Jacky'd say. 'That's eight bob, ' Kale'd say.

"'Well, Jacky, here's another item, ' Kale'd say. 'You got five bob on the twentyfirst? '—'Yes. ' 'Well, that's five bob you got, an' five bob you didn't get, eh? '—'That right. ' 'Well, that's ten bob, ' Kale'd say.

"'On the thirtieth y' got a dozen o' matches, ' Kale'd say. —'Yes, that right, ' Jacky'd say. 'That's a dozen y' got, an' a dozen y' didn't get, ain't it now? '—'Yes, that right, Mista Kale, ' Jacky'd say.

"'Well, that's nineteen bob, ain't it? '—'Yes, that right. ' 'Well here's th' balance, Jacky. Don't get drunk on it, ' Kale'd say—an' gave the pore dam nigger a bob. The black boy'd wonder how it was he never seemed to have anything owing to him, but he was too 'plurry plash' to let on he didn't know all about it.

"Now, all niggers are too 'plurry plash, ' so I carn't make out w'y the English Government gives these drivers on our transport four-ten a month w'en they could get 'em for a quid, an' dust 'em down over that too. Y' mus' keep niggers down. If y' let a nigger think he's 's good's a white man, y' can't do nothing with him.

"Now, there's that cove Frank on our cart. All that push that play cards under the cart of a night lets him chip in. They say to him: 'Y' black swine! '—an' he answers back an' calls 'em 'white swine, ' an' they on'y laugh. Frank was goin' inter Bloemfontein one day, an' he met a bloke from the 'Carles, ' an' seys, 'Hullo, you white swine! ' So the bloke from the 'Carles' up an' knocks him down. I reckon Frank was never more s'prised in his life. He jus' lay there hollerin', an' singing out: 'All right, baas, I didn't say it again, I didn't say it again'. But it was their fault—those coves that'd encouraged him to reckon he could chaff any white — —" and so forth.

You may light your pipe before turning in, if you like, provided that you do not make too great a glare of light. You must cover your head with the blanket when you strike the match. What a blessed thing tobacco is, after you have got past the first sharp stage of hunger! If you smoke a pipe, and tighten your belt a hole or two, you may imagine you have eaten a good dinner—supposing you have a very vivid imagination.

Soon every one on the post is sleeping the deep, wholesome sleep of the thoroughly tired. You go to bed with your bandolier on, and your carbine close at hand, on outpost. Neither do you remove boots or spurs. The sentry on the horse lines walks up and down, and prays for relief.

Down where the other sentries are it is very still and lonely. Of all the occupations of active service to which the private soldier is liable, there is none so arduous and responsible as that of a sentry on the line of outposts. He is in the front rank of the army. Nothing lies between him and the enemy. On his alertness rest the safety and the lives of his comrades. They may only sleep securely if he be wakeful and watchful. If he sleep, if he relax in his vigilant outlook he endangers not only his own worthless self, but his comrades in the outpost, the Brigade behind him, the Army itself—even the Empire, when it only needs another reverse or two to draw the intervention of a foreign power.

There is no offence in the calendar of soldier's crimes more heinous or far-reaching in its possible consequences than a sentry's neglect of his duty. No punishment can be too great for the man who sleeps upon his post. There can be no excuse, no extenuating circumstances. Even should he be kept awake for seven nights in succession, he should be shot without mercy if he slumber on the eighth, whilst a sentry in a responsible position. One may be sorry for him. His may be the hardest and most pitiable case in the world, but his punishment should be death—not so much because of the actual personal offence of which he has been guilty, as for an example to deter other men from doing likewise.

And, strange as it may seem, this is the actual view of nearly every soldier in the army. There was a story at Modder River of a man who slumbered on his post and was awarded seven years' gaol, whilst his friends—the men of his own regiment—clamoured for his death.

A sentry who sleeps on his post has committed the unpardonable sin. On the other hand, it is almost as criminal for a commanding officer to detail men who have not recently had a fair amount of rest for this onerous duty as it is for the sentry to sleep. Sentry-duty should not come more frequently than once in three nights.

You begin your watch heavy with sleep. That is the dangerous period, when you are most liable to yield. You hear the sergeant and the man whose place you have taken 'swish-swishing' through the grass back to the post. You are hardly awake yet. The sergeant has warned you not to stand upright as a mark for possible 'snipers, ' but you feel yourself that to sit down would be almost to court slumber. So you walk up and down, with your carbine at the 'support' across your body, and your face turned Boerwards half-interestedly. You stumble over tussocks of grass and bump into ant-hills, and wonder vaguely why you are there and whether the time will pass quickly until your turn comes for more sleep. By-and-bye a realisation that the night is cold, and sharp, and frosty thoroughly awakens you.

The moon, well in its third quarter, is flooding all the veldt with its silvery illusive light. The long kopje looms up under it—black, mysterious, ominous. Away, very far away in the distance, the range of hills you had seen when scouting this afternoon—or was it yesterday afternoon? —rises, light-bathed and ethereal, out of a low-lying sea of faint white mist. To the rear, a few thinly twinkling points of light mark a wing of the British camp—Hutton's Brigade probably. You cannot see your own. The outpost is not visible either from where you are. On your right, a tiny black spot shows the position of the other sentry. The uncanny stillness of the night gets on to your nerves. You feel terribly alone.

You see something dark and dim out in the long grass. It is vague, ill-defined, shadowy. What can it be? For a moment it looks like a crouching man. You half-expect the flash of a rifle and the sing of a bullet. You watch, and watch, and strain your eyes with watching—until they fill with tears, and you have to rub them clear again. There is another one five yards away, and another to the other side, and another, and another—a whole line of silently advancing Boers!

How uncertain this moonlight is! Is it time to fire? If one could only consult with the other sentry about them. What is he doing? The silly fool seems to be just walking up and down. Can't he see them? Won't it be better to shoot first and challenge after?

The long range of hills afar off flickers, and curls and warps up into the sky as your eyes swim again. They must be men, but why don't they advance, or fire, or do something?

You kneel down in the grass and rest your carbine over an ant-hill, and then you silhouette the square top of a stone fence-post against the sky, and wonder why you didn't think of it before, and the other Boers evolve themselves into stone fence-posts too.

Half an hour must be gone by now—no, three-quarters. It seems ages since the sergeant went away. If one could only do something to keep back the sleepiness. It is cold sitting down, too. You get up and walk again.

How about a smoke? Risky, reprehensible—but you must have one. It doesn't do to show a light towards the outpost, lest the lieutenant see you and become annoyed. It won't do to show one to the front, lest the Boers be close at hand and fire possible volleys. So you fill your pipe—a difficult matter when your fingers are frozen stiff. What of matches? There are some loose in your haversack—the last of their kind. They are wooden ones, but you have a bit of striking paper from the side of the box stowed away in your helmet. You crouch down behind an ant-heap. Then you lay your helmet on the ground with the apex pointing to your front. Unbuttoning your overcoat, you pull the collar up over your head. Kneeling, you strike the match in the helmet, and puff vigorously at the pipe. With your hand over the bowl, you rise up cautiously. The white smoke curls up into the frosty moonlight. You feel more wakeful and content.

It must be freezing now. Down in Bloemfontein people had said, "Wait until you start again in the winter. That's when you'll feel it. Why, half the army will be frozen to death before you cross the Vaal—and when you do cross it, and get into the High Veldt, you won't be able to live for cold. " And it is cold. But gloriously healthy. Use accustoms you to it. Were one sleeping in a warm house every night, it would be suicide, almost, to lie out with only one thin blanket in these white frosts, but after three or four months of roofless, open-air living it is no great hardship. Except when it rains.

Something is coming over the veldt up on your left—two men on horseback, talking together in low tones. The patrol coming in. Up they ride to within fifty yards of you. You challenge: "Halt! who goes there? "—"Friends. " "Advance one and give the countersign. " One of them rides slowly on, the other remaining where he is. "Pelican, " says the corporal; "warm weather, ain't it? " His companion rides past, and they return to the outpost. You envy them.

Tommy Cornstalk

Amongst the many stories which one heard of a certain well-advertised London volunteer corps, it was related that a member of it, being on 'sentry-go, ' was approached in the 'wee sma' hours' by his commanding officer. The sentry was not able, by reason of an impediment in his speech, to challenge properly. "S-t-t-op! w-h-o-'s that? " he inquired nervously. "Friend, " came the reply. "M-m-m-well, c-ccome up to the counter, and sign"!

In the fulness of time, after you have been thinking that all upon the post are asleep, and yourself a fixture until morning, you descry the relief coming out. You challenge, and get the countersign as a matter of form, and then go back to your downy couch. If you haven't taken the precaution to cover up your blanket with the waterproof sheet, you will find it wet with frost when you crawl beneath it.

Four more hours, and you are out again. It seems like five minutes since you came in. Your first watch was from ten o'clock until twelve. You have slept from midnight to four in the morning. And the end of this two hours brings you to the new day. You are relieved just in time to roll your coat and replace it upon the saddle, and to adjust your blanket and waterproof sheet. No time to light fires—the Brigade is moving early. So, if you possess a biscuit, you eat it as you prepare to move off, and mount and ride again upon an unfed horse—which is the 'crown of a sorrow's sorrow'.

Once an outpost of Australians were doing duty near Boesman's Kop by Bloemfontein. There were no rations, nor any apparent prospect of any. A cow at daylight passed close by a sentry on her way to water at a dam. A happy thought came to him—that cow was probably a Boer. So he decided to take no risks, and shot her dead. There were rations that day. They came from the cow, in the shape of beefsteaks. How was the sentry to know, when the cow didn't answer his challenge, that she was not a kind of 'wooden horse of Troy'? He could risk no surprises.

CHAPTER VI - THE BIVOUAC

This morning the place was bare, and empty, and desolate, save for the white farmhouse beside the great stone-banked dam—and it added, if anything, to the desolation.

Some 'Jan' or 'Piet' had come galloping across the veldt at noon with news of oncoming rooineks, who poured over the country like a swarm of locusts, eating up and devouring everything that lay in its path—ruthless, overpowering, merciless alike to women, and children, and aged people.

They were so many nothing could stand against them. Their shrapnel searched every kopje and cluster of rocks. They had left the railway, and were sweeping on alone in the open veldt. It was not true that the Englishmen got lost and died when they went away from the railway. It was not true that they had used up all the horses from England before they had come to Bloemfontein. All those men had horses—many horses, and waggons, and cannon. Yesterday they had fired a Maxim-Nordenfeldt into Sarel Du Ploy's garden, and had killed Tantie Du Ploy's best cow.

It was not true that they had no Maxim-Nordenfeldts. They had one, at any rate, for a little devil had cut his hat's rim—here, at the side. See it!

Tantie must trek. The Kaffirs must inspan the oxen. There was no time. Even now, their scouts were not two hours away. Yes, yes—she must go. Would she wait to be misused by these 'verdomde rooineks'? Would she wish to see her babies tossed on the spear-heads of the wicked lancers, her home rent, and riven, and burnt over her head?

White flags! What of white flags? They no longer cared about them. Why, they had had three of them over Du Ploy's chimneys when they fired upon the English scouts—and yet the little devils of Maxim-Nordenfeldts had come—crack-crackcrack—into the garden, and they had had to run like Kaffirs to get away from them. The Englishmen had become 'slim' themselves in the matter of white flags. Last week a lyddite bomb had blown to pieces Hans Larsen and his son, as they fired from a kraal over which they had taken the precaution to mount a white shirt. No, she must not talk—she must trek.

It is that 'kerel' French who is coming, and, almighty, but he comes quickly, and no one knows whence. He must be off soon to warn others. Let her inspan at once. It was no time for waiting.

And the poor woman has inspanned, and piled her best belongings, with her babies, on the waggons; and has gone, white-faced but unweeping, before the vague terror of the accursed rooinek, whom, the predicant has told her, knows no respect for wife, or maiden, or mother, or little child. And to-night her house shelters a General of Division.

From the little farm it must seem a strangely altered scene this evening. Where, at sunrise, a few oxen grazed quietly, and were the only living things for many miles, the veldt is covered by a great gathering of men and horses. Away to the left, the blue smoke of another great camp hangs like a thin veil above the land, and, back in the rear, there is another brigade guarding the immense convoy which keeps on coming in until long after dark.

Our own camp is half a mile long or more; and nearly as deep as long, with its guns, and waggons, and red cross ambulances. Mules linked together in fours and fives are being driven to water by yelling and screaming Kaffir boys. The far side of the big dam in the hollow is fringed with drinking, bare-backed horses. Wild-looking men in khaki chase squawking fowls about the huts of the Kaffir farm-servants. An unkempt ruffian in a torn shirt is cutting the throat of a squealing pig behind the house. Horses are tied to the big willow tree.

Red lapelled staff officers come and go from the front rooms. Now and then a dapper little man in yellow riding boots walks out upon the stoep, and says something that causes men to spring to take papers from his hand, and mount, and ride away at breakneck speed. An anxious-looking colonel dismounts stiffly from his horse, hands the reins to a trumpeter who has come with him, and walks inside. Soon he reappears with the dapper General, talking quickly in a low voice. The General holds a half-unrolled map in his hand. He spreads it out on his knee, uses his forefinger as an emphatic pointer, and appears to be insisting upon something. The colonel smiles and nods, and seems to have comprehended. Whereat the little red-faced, stout man is apparently pleased. He goes inside again with a cheery "All-right. Good-night. " Johnny French must have another of those wonderful movements of his simmering in his brain.

Somehow, French doesn't strike you with any idea of his being the smart man he is—except when you notice the shrewd, twinkling little eyes that seem to take in everything about him. He certainly does not look the ideal cavalry leader. There is nothing of the Brigadier Gerard in his appearance. Short, dumpy, jaunty—sitting a horse rather like the proverbial sack o' flour; if you saw him booted and spurred in Cape Town you would almost put him down as a colonel of infantry, who had learned to ride from a Red-Book in a riding-school at considerable pains. And yet, they say he is a hunting man, and rides straight enough. In dress and person he is always neat. When you salute him he returns it courteously with a smiling face. When he finds fault there is, one hears, no mistaking his meaning. Staff-signallers will tell you that his vocabulary does not lack of means of emphasis. They relate a tale of how he had once spoken to a luckless Brigadier who had contrived to mask the guns of 'French's Pets' in a certain action, and it was said that the recipient of his address seemed to pray for the advent of a six-inch shell by way of a change of subject. It was probably not true, but they report him to have inquired sarcastically as to whether the Brigadier was of any possible use whatever, whether he could lead ducks any better than he could lead cavalry, and to have finished with a simple statement to the effect that the youngest subaltern in the other Brigade could lead that of the gentleman in question better far than he could himself.

He is a wonderful little man. Except in the one matter of considering that horses are made of iron and can thrive better on long and rapid marches than on oats, his men give him credit for never making a mistake. The trust and pride of the private soldier of his Division in his infallibility and achievements pass all understanding. Whatever may be the work in hand, every one feels absolutely confident that, though it may not always succeed as fully as expected, it will never be bungled so long as 'Johnny' has control of it. And if, in any of the towns, the surrendered Boers should ask you whom you serve under, and you reply, "French, " they will gape at you as being something above the common run of 'rooineks'.

He has acquired an almost demoniac reputation amongst the Boers for being able to be in two places at once. "What is the use? " they say. "We dig trenches, and place cannon, and keep the khakis back for hours; and with our spy-glasses we think we see his cavalry lurking behind—but, presently, round he comes on our line of retreat, and we are obliged to trek quickly, lest we be caught and hemmed in, as was Cronje at Paardeberg. "

In the lines the horses are eating their evening oats, and the men all busy cooking. It is a curiously interesting and picturesque scene.

When you look at a bivouac at night Modern War loses its modernity. Smokeless powder, seven-mile ranges, unseen death—all the adjuncts of our civilised methods of settling disputes are hidden away in the darkness. There are only the little twinkling fires, the tired horses, the hungry men, the smell of cooking, the quiet voices and the laughter and snatches of song just as it might have been a thousand years ago. Whether men kill one another with axes or with magazine rifles, they are still men. They must sleep, and eat, and be cold. The English camp on the night before Agincourt couldn't have been very much different to this in appearance. It makes you feel somehow that, after all, we haven't improved very much in the centuries. There are railways, and steamships, and electricity, and adequate drainage in cities, and 'heaps' of other ways of making life more healthy and agreeable—but, in the end, when we want to settle a question between individuals or nations we come back to our own nature, and settle it still after the manner of the beasts of the field and the fowl of the air.

There are three regiments, with from three to four squadrons apiece, in the Brigade, and a battery of Horse Artillery. Each regiment is in 'mass' formation with regard to its squadrons—that is to say the leading troop of the squadron is on the front line, and the others behind it, in succession, to the rear—so that the squadrons lie side by side, and are of about the same depth. Every horse is allowed sufficient space to ensure him non-interference on the part of his neighbour. Between the parallel squadrons a narrow street is left. Between the regiments the streets are a little wider. Behind each squadron is its transport, and behind that again the transport of the regiment as a whole. In rear of all are the Army Service waggons, and a little way aside of them the ambulance vans neatly dressed in line The battery is usually on the right of the Brigade—with its guns and ammunition-waggons in rear. Seen from a distance, the whole seems to be a little more than a large cluster of men, horses, guns and waggons, jumbled together anyhow—but when you come closer you will see that all is duly ordered, that everything has its place and allotted position.

Almost in front of all are the little 'one man' green and white tents of the officers, and just beyond them the headquarters of the Brigade, where good 'Uncle Tom'—most popular of Brigadiers—shows his red lamp o' nights.

The dingy saddles and arms are arrayed in order—each saddle before its horse, and the whole line 'dressed' correctly. It is only a 'one night' camp, and so there are not many of the tiny blanket-dwellings—built with swords and carbines and bridlereins—such as spring up when the march is checked for a day or two. Men are moving about with jackets unbuttoned and puttees removed, and are a motley, shabby crowd enough.

Dreadful to contemplate, horrible to relate, but necessary to mention if one would seek to give a truthful picture of the minor aspects of a campaign, are the efforts of mankind in African warfare to rid themselves of the loathsome vermin which infest clothing and blankets and person, and every moment of existence. It is a shocking state of affairs, and few escape—even though there are some who will not acknowledge its existence, as far as they themselves are concerned. One consolation men offered themselves—that the plague was of the veldt, and therefore unavoidable.

Insecticide is no good. Neither do cleanly habits mitigate the evil. There is but one means of keeping down the population. You must hunt, and you must kill. And so, when you behold half-naked men seated upon their kits, earnestly and laboriously scanning their shirts, and grunting with satisfaction at intervals, you will understand what it means. When a column halts in the afternoon in order to bivouac for the night, one of the first things infested men do is to squat down on the ground, pull off their shirts, and seek what they may find.

One feels almost apologetic for having written of such a subject, but it is just as much a feature of warfare as are battles—more so, even, than battles, for the battles are simply occasional episodes, but the 'Scots Greys, ' or 'Roberts' Horse, ' as they have been almost universally termed, like the poor, are always with you.

The name bestowed upon these awful insects is not complimentary to the Second Dragoons—but it may have been the motto of that gallant regiment—'Second to None'—which suggested the comparison to the original libeller. The 'Greys' of the veldt are certainly 'second to none'.

Fuel was always a problem. If you could get a post, or half a post, you were indeed fortunate. It meant comparative luxury. You might cook—supposing there was anything to be cooked—and after that you could sit round the tiny blaze and feel that there really was some comfort left in the world after all. It was cheerful, even, to look at the warm glow of two little burning sticks. Sometimes you got part of a door, or a window-sash, or a flooring-board. A baby's cradle, the leg of a piano, a railway sleeper—anything that would burn was worth its weight in transport.

The Boers themselves depend for their fire on an evil composition known as 'mest'. It is essentially dried cattle dung, and you may see it in process of manufacture for the market in the Kaffir locations in any of the towns. They collect the raw material on the veldt, or in the cattle kraals, puddle it up in tubs with water, cut it into cakes, and stack it to dry in the sunlight. It is not the pleasantest thing in the world to cook with, but once alight it gives out a good heat, and in a country where wood is so scarce and valuable that stone posts are cheap for fencing, the possibility of obtaining even such a fuel as 'mest' is something to be thankful for.

Biscuit-boxes are excellent kindling fuel, but difficult to obtain, and transitory and uncertain in their effectiveness. Moreover, they are the peculiar perquisites of Quarter-master sergeants and cooks, and unless you are a gifted thief you are not frequently able to get away with them. Railway sleepers are solid and lasting, but, being saturated with tar, burn smokily and with prejudicial effect upon the taste of rations cooked in their flames.

Best of all are the wooden fence-posts. They are not 'split, ' but are the solid round trunks of blue gum saplings, and they burn with the fragrant scent you know so well—so that if you shut your eyes, as you sit round the fire smoking, visions of 'somewhere else' come to you dreamily across the months.

The Netherlands Railway—or, to be correct, the Corporation that branded its rolling-stock Z. A.R. S.M. (Zuid Afrikaansche Republiek

Spoorweg Maatschappij) thoughtfully fenced its permanent way with blue gum posts. There are none left along the line now. What few the invading army passed by on its way to Pretoria have been carefully culled by the subsequent patrols that rode between the little entrenched stations seeking dynamite cartridges. There were many posts on the farms. That was how you were able to judge whether a farm was fairly prosperous or not. You did not look for fat cattle or good crops. You sought wooden fence-posts. And when you beheld them you knew that the late occupant of the farm had been a member of the Volksraad, or a holder of Government concessions, or a Landrost. No one but a wealthy man can afford to fence with wooden posts in South Africa. And they were truly a Godsend to Tommy Atkins and Tommy Cornstalk. If, towards evening, when there seemed to be a prospect of getting into quarters for the night before very long, a Brigade should happen to encounter a line of wire fencing with wooden posts, such event was hailed with the utmost joy and gratitude. Lines of men spread along it on either side of the direction of the march, and, by the time that the last waggon had rattled through the opening made by the wire-cutters, there was no fence remaining for a mile or two to left and right. Should the march not come to an end so soon as expected, men often carried heavy posts on their shoulders or across their wallets, for hours and miles. Any labour was worth undertaking for a fire at night.

A six-pound bully-beef tin is an excellent and providential article of veldt culinary ware. You pick it up empty at daylight in the lines, and fasten it to the end of your carbine-bucket, where, during the day, it plays a picturesque and not unmusical part. At nightfall, after you are fed, you fill it with water and boil the fat and dust out of it on your fire, and you possess an invaluable utensil. You may carry water in it, or you may draw your tea and coffee in it, or you may boil down your scraggy beef, or make a curry, or a rice pudding, or the satisfying and sustaining mealie-pap. At a pinch, you may use its flat side as a writing-desk.

The cavalry mess-tin is a poor thing—a simple frying-pan of shallow make, designed rather to hang easily from the saddle than to possess any intrinsic merit as a cooking-pot—but the infantry tin, that is indeed a friend of man. It does not carry well on horseback. It is built to sit upon the rolled blanket which the foot soldier bears in the 'small' of his overladen back; but of all useful, convenient, adaptable, blessed contrivances it is surely a prince among pots. About seven inches long and four wide, it is oval on the one side and flat upon the other. It is a little deeper than wide. There is a handle to the body by which you may lift it on or off the fire. Its lid is a frying-pan whose handle folds within, and a tin plate is fitted ingeniously into the top of the pot. You may boil your mealies and fry your steak at the same time, and when you have eaten the former to the last vestige, you may draw your coffee in it. Truly, it comes next to the cavalry cloak as a good and sensible piece of equipment. No kit, as an advertisement would say, is complete without one.

Night comes down over the great camp—sudden, black, cold. The little fires twinkle through the legs of horses. Over in the Artillery lines a great group of overcoats stands out against a brighter blaze. The gunners are burning a Boer waggon and giving a concert. Queer barrack-room ballads—just as Kipling renders them, only more so— are roared out into the night.

Git up, you ord'ly man!

Git up, you ord'ly man!

Carn't you 'ear the ord'ly sargint call-in'? Git up an' clean th' room,

Or the clink'll be y'r doom—

Y'll be up before old Squidgy in the morn-in'.

Their songs have many verses, and many quaint features, but they are not the kind of songs which would be popular at tea-meetings. There is a gracefully graceless ribaldry about the majority of them that keeps them also from ever getting written.

There was a mess of four in that bivouac—and in many other bivouacs of that march to Pretoria. Sometimes it shared two biscuits and a little raw beef, sometimes it fared sumptuously on the best that the land had to give. To-night heaven had sent a Canadian. He had ridden jauntily into the lines, inquiring for his 'outfit'—which was the Second Canadian M. I. No one knew where the Canadian M. I. might be. The night was black as ink, and seemed to threaten rain.

"Say, " said the 'Yank, ' "kin I throw down with you boys, then? Guess you are the Australians, ain't that so? Waal, if I carn't find any more Canadians, I reckon th' Australians comes pretty close up. Y' don't mind if I throw down in this hyar lo-cation, do yew now? Guess I kin contribute my share to the festive board. "

We knew not the verb 'to throw down'—but, as two fowls hung to one side of his queer saddle and a leg of mutton to the other, we intimated that he might, if he chose, do as he desired.

So he 'threw down'—that is to say, he untied the various knots of buffalo-hide and string which kept the saddle in its place, picketed the remarkably fresh pony in the lines, and disposed of his blanket and coat amongst our kits. And we assisted in the cooking of the poultry and the mutton, as well as in the eating thereof, and they were very good, and after they were all gone except the bones and the feathers, we were able to supply him with some real tobacco to chew. You cannot chew Boer tobacco.

So, whilst the thin smoke of our pipes lost itself amongst the stars, and the little flickering flame at the end of the fence-post lit up bearded and dirty, but no longer hungry faces, an hour or two passed pleasantly enough in yarns, and lies, and lazy anecdotes. One spoke of cane growing on the Northern River, and waxed enthusiastic over the great forests, and the red cedar, and the soil. Another became eloquent as to lucerne on the Hunter. Another lied of little fish that came out of artesian bores where he lived. Another, who was an Irishman and a policeman, recounted some few of his adventures and misadventures whilst in charge of a lunatic on the Macleay.

The Canadian chewed and spat royally into the fire until it was in danger of extinguishment, and told us of his doings of the day.

"Now, I'll jes' tell yew boys what one of those something French's Scouts had the darned hide to do, or raither to try to do, during the day. I reckon he had a pretty con-siderable section of real, slap-up cheek, too.

"Y' see, two of the boys, and yours truly, we slipped away from th' 'outfit' t' see what we could pick up sorter permiscuous like. We moosied along over the darned veldt until we came to a Kaffir kral— a pretty good kind of kral, too—mud cabin an' bamboo fixin's. Must'er b'longed to pretty w'althy col'd gent, I guess. And we sees a lot of ponies browsin' roun' in th' prairie. After a deal of trouble, we corralled the mustangs in one of them stone corrals, an' calc'lated to fix ourselves with re-mounts and a spare hoss or two to lead along to the 'outfit'. So we sot down to make a pot of tea, before catching the ponies an' gettin' along.

"Bymbye, up comes a leftenint of French's Scouts, with a yaller boy ridin' behind him, a-leadin' his pack-horse. An' he sees our re-mounts. So, without so much as having the po-liteness to ask for one, he sails in an' commences to help himself to the pick of our private stud. We watched him select his fancy—an' he took a deal of care in pickin' it out. One o' th' boys re-marks to him: 'Say, mister, what are y' calc'latin' to do with that there pony y' got roped up thar?' He allowed he was goin' t' have it. 'Oh, no,' my friend sez, quiet like; 'oh, no, y'r not—they jes' about b'long to me 'n my friends here.' 'My deah fellow,' sez French's Scout, 'they do not. They b'long to the Kaffirs, and I'm goin' ter requisition this one. I'm an off'cer,' he sez; 'I hold Her Majesty's commission.' 'Waal,' sez Charley, 'y' might hold th' angel Gabriel's co-mission, an' then agin', y' mightn't,' he sez; 'but I guess y' jes' goin' t' leave that darned hoss whar he is. We've taken the trouble to run them in,' he sez, 'and we jes' about con-clude that they are our private prop'ty. An' what's more,' he sez, 'I guess y'r lookin' f'r trouble,' he sez, 'an' I kin tell yew y've come right har whar you kin git it!' he sez.

"An' at last we con-vinced him that our title was O. K., an' he left in a dam hurry to see the provo'-marshal about it.

"But this here's what stuck in my neck—his own hoss was good, an' fresh, an' fit for anything, but he wanted to take one of our re-mounts to give to his nigger—yes, gentlemen, to his darned useless nigger! If his own hoss had bin knocked up, we'd bin happy to sell him one, supposin' he'd asked f'r it civil and nice, but he ackshally—true's I'm sittin' right har—he wanted to give one of our hosses to his darned Jim Crow coon! We couldn't 'low that, so we hunted him an' his darned son of a sweep away."

As you make your bed so you must lie upon it. If you wake up in the night with an impression of lying across a small kopje it is quite your own fault. You should have kicked down the tussocks and removed the loose stones before you spread out the waterproof sheet.

There is a good deal of art required in the making of a comfortable bed if your only material consists of a mackintosh sheet, one brown blanket and an overcoat. On these frosty nights you have to get the maximum of warmth out of the minimum of material. You pull the saddle round so that its seat faces the direction of the wind, and stand it up on end so that the sideflaps make a small shelter for your head. Inside the saddle you make your pillow out of haversack, towel, helmet—anything available that may serve your needs best. To undress, you remove your spurs and boots, and unwind the puttees from your legs. If you wrap your feet up in your puttees they will keep them warm, but the best plan is to leave your boots on, and pull a pair of woollen socks over them—provided, of course, that you possess the socks. You lie down upon the waterproof sheet, pull the blanket up to your ears, and spread out the coat sideways over it. Then you tuck blanket and coat round your feet and under your sides, pull the thrice-blessed 'Balaclava' over your ears, light your pipe, and thank heaven fervently for the many luxuries it is your privilege to enjoy.

It is a queer life this. No one at home can know it exactly as it is. No one out here can quite describe it. It is rough, it is hard and it is dangerous, but it is intensely interesting and exciting. The glorious healthiness of it is its perfect charm. There are fever, and dysentery, and pneumonia—but, provided that you can keep clear of these, you will almost fatten on it. There is also, of course, considerable danger of what a certain member of the much-quoted quoted Canadians termed 'darned leadpoisoning'—meaning thereby, the chance of going under to a bullet—but that is the element which supplies the excitement, and, as a matter of fact, is far less a real danger than the bad water and insanitary surroundings.

War may be immoral, and deplorable, and barbarous, but from the point of view of the combatant (not the women and children) there are many worse phases of existence. It is a big sport, a gamble with fate—and, as such, while the human composition remains human, it will never cease to exercise a certain fascination and attractiveness to man.

CHAPTER VII - THE BATTLE

The long rocky ridges overlooking the road down which the Boer convoy disappeared at dusk last evening is a bleak, windswept, unhappy place at dawn. It has been an unhappy place all through the long darkness—a lonely, inhospitable, barren perch upon which lost souls might roost and bemoan their fates in the small hours and be in keeping with their surroundings, but where flesh and blood feels that it is distinctly a trial of patience and endurance to spend eight freezing hours.

All night the bitter wind has whined and whistled through the rocks, moaning sadly in the long dry grass and about the scanty bushes, thrusting its icy hand into one's very body through cloak, and tunic, and jumper, and woollen shirt. To stand upon the summit keeping watch had been as though one walked naked along the weather side of a ship's deck in Southern seas. The clear brightness of the stars blazing and twinkling in a cloudless sky overhead has accentuated the keen chill of existence on this iceberg, glacier, snowfield— anything but good, dry, warm, hospitable earth.

At dusk, our rifles had flamed long-range volleys into the valley, and we had prayed for just one little field-gun, for just one handy Maxim to reach the crawling oxen, that slowly and haltingly, but bravely and surely, dragged the last of the Boers' waggons into safety and escape behind the little rise that covered their crossing to the river. We had been too few to make the sudden dash that would have given them to us, too far ahead of the slow batteries that might have wrecked and splintered wheels and disselbooms and covers, and mowed down the patient oxen where they toiled laboriously to shelter. One Maxim might have done it. One pom-pom would have captured them at five thousand yards, but our little carbines could not check the slow escape at half that distance.

Once, as the last waggon came slowly into the field of fire, it had halted and remained. Through glasses, the spit of the hailing nickel had made on the ground about it a little dust squall. Two yoke of oxen fell before it, and the cart seemed to be over. Yet brave men had come through the storm of death leading slow oxen, and had gallantly drawn the waggon the hundred yards that had to be crossed before it disappeared from out straining eyesight in the fast gathering gloom. Brave, dauntless, determined men those—whether sjambok-threatened Kaffirs or plucky Boers—and one could hardly hold back a cheer even, as the almost abandoned team crawled into safety round the shoulder of the tiny hillock.

The Boer may be an unenlightened, slothful 'waster'. He may not have too well-defined notions as to treachery and guile. He may play the white flag trick—but he is no coward. Black-hearted Ben Viljoen had led a team of horses to save a pom-pom on the Tugela, alone and single-handed, and had saved it, and been credited with his brave deed; but that Boer or Kaffir driver who brought the slow bullocks into the rain of bullets in the cold dusk of that winter evening by the Gatsrand did something which, had it been a gun and he an Englishman, would have won for him the V. C. and a justly and well earned fame. In point of merit it was a deed no whit behind the saving of the guns of 'Q' Battery at Sanna's Post. Heaven alone knows now what the cart contained. Had it been bar-gold instead of possible mealies, or shells, or furniture, its salvation from us could not have been more worthy of respect, or more admirable and gallant than it was.

Here, at daylight, as the cold sky paled and yellowed and flamed into the crimson promise of a glorious day, we sat among the rocks and shivered. The ridge we had occupied through the night sloped, not very steeply, up from the valley we had been ascending all yesterday afternoon, but dropped in a sudden steepness below us into as fair a vale as ever man had gazed upon.

A tree-lined river meandered down a flat. White farms dotted its banks, and little plots of 'cultivation'. Beyond it stretched a grassy plain to the low, rocky foothills of a line of purple ranges over which towered one great berg higher than its fellows. All about the horizon weird spidery structures with tall smoke stacks stood out black and sharply cut against the fresh sky. Over all brooded the calm of early morning—the quiet peacefulness of a world not yet awake.

It was the promised land, the lost Eldorado of so many months which had been the ultimate cause of our coming from all the quarters of the globe—the rich, blood-bought gold-reef, which, argue as we may concerning the enlightenment we distribute with bullet and lyddite, or the visions of Dutch confederation which Paul Kruger and Steyn, his dupe, might have dreamed, was, and is, the great final casus belli of this bloody struggle between Dutch and English for supremacy in South Africa.

One could not gaze out over the quiet valley and beyond the dim ridges to where the great mine buildings stood—some of them still sending up thin columns of black smoke into the clear air, and still seeming to be worked—without feeling that here, at last, was the thing we had been marching, and starving, and getting fever, and dying for all these months past; that here, indeed, was the great reward of toil, and danger, and sickness, and blood that had been spilt as water over half a year and more. This was the thing that was to pay for Magersfontein, and Colenso, and Stormberg, and the Tugela—for the sufferings of the women and little children of Ladysmith, and Kimberley, and Mafeking. Here it was—a long system of a particular kind of dirt, occurring in a peculiar geological fashion and containing a yellow metal. This was the prize, the great bone of contention which the big dog was taking from the little one—and taking it simply because he could not avoid doing so.

O land of gold and greed, mysterious lying and open cheating, how much have you to answer for! The burned homes, the bullet-pocked walls, the new graves, the pestilential hospitals, the brave lives—how great and strong for good you will need to become ere you pay for all these! Treasure, and Life, and Love. These are the items of your vast indebtedness, and the last not the least. Do you think, Golden Rand, that you will ever liquidate your liabilities?

Over there, vaguely beyond the ranges, lies Johannesburg. Somewhere not very far across the veldt the ill-starred Jameson brought his idiotic raid to an inglorious finish. What a finish—we have not come to it yet.

The sun rises out of the shoulder of the great berg. There are no Boers in all the valley. Everything is still and tranquil, as it always should be in this vale of peace. From the farmhouses on the river bends the blue smoke curls up into the morning. Cocks crow distantly below our feet. The road that leads behind the little hillock stretches clear and white from out the narrow pass on our left hand. There is no sign or trace of the convoy that trekked along it yesternight, save a couple of black specks very far away that may be dead oxen.

They have all gone apparently—gone again as always. We march, and march, and march day after day, week after week, and we never come to handgrips with our wily foe. Will they ever stand and fight us? Will they ever give us the chance we want so badly of bringing the war to an end in one grand death-grip? Are we always to trek, trek, trek till the Day of Judgment, and never catch and close with them? Will they defend the city?

What a joke it would be to shell Johannesburg! From all accounts it would be a glorious place to wreck. And then—the loot. Think of it, you who own it—how would it be if we, the saviours of your dividends, had had to blast your assets with common shell. Our stars—but it would have been funny! Mayfair, Rondebosch, Durban, Delagoa—how you would have squirmed as you read. It would well-nigh have been as comfortable for you in the cold veldt, where you would, at least, have had the distraction of doing, as to be biting your nails and fuming impotently over the wires that told of your stores, and banks, and suburbs under the blighting influence of the Four-point-Sevens.

The sun rose higher. Up on the ridge the wind that blew all night had stopped the frost, but down in the sheltered shadow of the hills it covered the grass in great patches like thin snow. The cold breeze had died away at dawn, and now, though still bitterly raw to half-starved men, the day was slowly brightening and mellowing in the golden sunlight.

They were strange figures that huddled amongst the rocks. Unshaven, dirty, wolfish faces looked grimly out from woollen caps and mufflers as the tired men sat in their blue-black overcoats, with the great collars sticking up about their ears, carbines resting across knees, the thin reek of disreputable pipes tingeing the clear air.

Last night had been supperless. No one knew where the Brigade might be, save that it had halted somewhere behind in yesterday's valley. We could not see back to overlook it because the ridge was flat on top, and wide ere it fell away. The horses had remained at the foot with their holders all night. We had had no blankets, nothing to eat or drink, and there was going to be no breakfast. The day was bright enough, and the sky blue, and the view magnificent—but how may you appreciate a fine day, and an azure sky, and a glorious prospect when there is nothing in your inside but a hollow?

A man came up on the ridge who said we were to rejoin the Brigade and draw more ammunition. Had he mentioned biscuits or bully-beef he would have been appreciated and popular. As it was, the message he brought got him disliked. We had emptied our bandoliers into the convoy last evening, so that the order to replenish them out of the ammunition-cart hardly augured anything out of the common.

We gathered up haversacks and water-bottles, and wended our weak way down the slope to where the poor limp horses and the profane horse-holders hung their heads and cursed the cold night respectively.

The Brigade had camped below the ridge. The Fourth were across the valley, upon the other side of the pass, and Hutton's Mounted Infantry were tumbling along with their guns from behind. The long train of transport-waggons toiled up the valley.

When the little packets had been untied, and the slim cartridges stowed away in the bandoliers, we mounted and rode back to a farmhouse in the rear, where there was a dam, in order to water the horses. There was absolutely nothing left at that farm except some hay, which a foraging Cornstalk had discovered in a loft—hundreds of bundles of it. Fowls, pigs, sheep—everything—had been eaten up over night; so we watered our horses, and strapped two bundles of hay apiece to the rear of the saddles, and rode back to the Brigade, which was forming up to march.

Down through the narrow road between the hills the dingy column rolled heavily in the dust. Sweating engineers threw gravel and rocks into the ruts and ditches so that the jolting guns might pass by. Dragoons, Hussars, Cornstalks, Canadians chaffed, and spat, and smoked by the roadside. The cloud of fine white dust rose high into the air. If there were any Boers watching from the Berg they would know, without doubt, that the khakis were coming.

At the foot of the steep hills some sort of order evolved itself from chaos. Batteries pieced themselves together again. Harassed mules drew bumping Scotch carts to their rightful regiments. Troops, and squadrons, and regiments and brigades reformed.

The Fourth Brigade drew away to the left, and rode to find a crossing-place higher up the river. We went on down the road, past the hillock where the dead trek-oxen lay, and a little pool of dried blood had congealed by the side of the track—past a white house, and a garden, and a store on to a short wooden bridge that led across the little stream, and where the column narrowed into 'files' and crossed more slowly, the scouts spreading out and galloping over the plains beyond the farther bank.

The trees along the river were beautiful weeping willows, shady elms and great Cape-mulberries. Then the flat extended before us— waving grass that shone as a wheat-field in the morning sunlight— and stretched away to a low line of rocky kopjes immediately in front, and a short two miles away, sweeping round the left extremity of the tiny range and on up into low rolling ridges. Beyond the line of rocks towards which we moved there was another and a higher series, separated from the first by a gently rising plain. Beyond them, again, rose taller hills, and from their midst the great blue Berg dominated all, and seemed to frown upon us as we came riding over the plain.

The quiet glory of a divine day rested over everything. Doves cooed musically in the river timber, one red-brick house to the left nestled in a bend. Six tall poplars grew before it, bare and leafless now. The inevitable white flag flew from a chimney.

As we left the bridge and the river we spread out across the plain in long lines twenty yards apart. Each man was fifty from his right and left hand neighbour. Something was in the wind, but no one knew what. Perhaps Johnny French had known, and that was why we extended so rapidly to the most open of open order as we came on to the wide plain.

Until the guns open you never know that you are going into battle. So many times were the usual precautions against surprise taken by the leaders, and so many times did emptiness of event characterise the day's operations, that we had begun to be sceptical as to whether 'opening out' really meant anything or not—whether all preparation for possible combat were not, after all, a mere matter of form. There were, of course, signs and omens that might point to an engagement, as, for instance, when the 'Pick-me-ups' (ambulance waggons) followed close up to the firing line. But, as a rule, it was never safe to prophesy an action until the first Boer shell came howling overhead. Brer' Boer was so very much an adept at lyin' low an' sayin' nuffin' until the time came when he considered he might say it with most effect, that it frequently came about that you were in the midst of a hot fire although, half an hour before, you would have readily betted against any possibility of such an eventuality. And, just as frequently, after you had been cautiously 'feeling' some 'dirty' country for half an afternoon you would find that he was not there.

You are half across the plain now—riding loosely and carelessly through the rich grass, the hungry horses reaching greedily for a mouthful of it every now and then. The black dots of scouts have reached and passed the first line of rocks. They are in the little strip of open country between that ridge and the next.

Ping-pong!

"Hullo! what's that? " you ask yourself aloud, at the same time gathering up the loose reins and pulling your horse together. All eyes are straining after the specks that move across the open, but, as you ride forward, the ridge in front just hides them.

Ping-pong! ping-pong! ping, ping, ping-pong! pong, pong—p-r-r-r-r-r-mp! —pingpong! ping-pong! It is the overture. A running, ripping, far away crashing of rifle-fire comes from the second ridges. You cannot see the scouts, but you know how they are racing. They are getting it 'pretty hot, ' and somehow it seems to you rather funny.

Ah! Now it is our turn.

Far away, on the left shoulder of the great Berg, a little white cloud, wonderfully clear and distinct, has risen into the blue sky. You have seen it before—that beautiful, white, woolly cloud.

For a long time nothing seems to come of it. Five, ten, fifteen seconds slip by and the day is just as still, and calm, and beautiful as before. Twenty seconds—and a deep, solemn, reverberating 'boom-m' trembles through the clear air.

"It's close now. Is the dam thing coming my way? "

The great Creusot shell suddenly whistles and howls high overhead, and, almost as soon as you have heard it in the air, it bursts with a thunderous, sudden 'bang! ' that cuts short its devilish song, throwing up a great column of dust and dirt and stones behind you, and seeming to blow a man and a horse who are near it into a thousand pieces. Almost before the dust and blue smoke and smell of powder have drifted away you see that man pulling his astonished charger on to its feet again! The long lines of horse-men move slowly over the plain.

It is the first note of an infernal symphony which is to be played all day.

Again the solemn 'boom-m'—but this time from another place, and with no white cloud. Again the shrieking flutter in the sky, and again the crashing burst and flying stones—away to your left.

Still the steady lines move forward.

From the Berg the white tuft of smoke once more drifts up, slowly and peacefully, into the blueness. This time you count the seconds carefully. Between 'nineteen' and 'twenty' the great gun booms out its note to you.

There are no sound symbols to express that rushing, howling, whining whir-r-r, as the ninety-six pounds of destructiveness cleave their rapid, invisible way through the air—but it is a sound which you will never confuse with any other in your life.

The abrupt explosion again cuts it short. This one bursts just short of the leading line. You rapidly reckon up the range. Twenty seconds divided by five gives four. Roughly, you are four miles away from the black-powder Creusot. It is somewhere about seven thousand yards.

Good shooting! They have put in one just too far and another just too short. The next ought to do something.

Two more hurtling shots from the invisible Long Toms dig harmless holes in the veldt to left and right.

The whole plain is full of horsemen now. They come on—quietly, ordered, slow—towards the rocks. It is the wonder of discipline. Nobody enjoys being shelled. Every one would rather be somewhere else. It is no 'picnic' to behold sudden death arriving by the hundredweight. Hardest of all is it to walk your nervous horse, and to keep the intervals and 'dressing' of the open ranks so that you do not bunch. But just because that cool Colonel—who is as a gentle old lady in camp—gives no order and makes no sign you ride forward, a better man than in all your life before, because you have learned your lesson of blind obedience, even unto Death.

Some squadrons edge over to the open ground on the left that passes by the end of the ridge. We are evidently going to occupy those rocks.

The Berg puffs its smoke into the sky once again. Again the long waiting. Again the weird scream—and then—b-r-rump! bang! —the shell plumps right into the midst of the moving swarm of horsemen, a hundred yards to your right front and close beside a horse. Through the drifting dust and dull smoke you see him lifted off his legs backwards and thrown to the ground across his rider. You notice that a hind leg kicks feebly—once, twice—and is still. The man's head and shoulders are towards you. His left hand neighbour digs in the spurs, gallops suddenly to where the lifeless heap of man and horse lies in the grass beside a great new hole, and dismounts and bends over the stricken pair.

Suddenly his hand goes up, and he seems to have called, for another man races to the spot. Together they drag, and pull, and shove—and, ere you are past, one of them is supporting a reeling, drunken, limp-legged figure who is, mirabile dictu, yet alive—though he himself does not seem quite certain of the fact. He staggers back on foot, his comrades' arms about his shoulders, and sits down on the ground with his dazed head in his hands.

The fear of God is in your heart, but still you ride slowly forward.

From somewhere in the second line of rocks a new note reaches you. It is closer and louder, and so close that you are able to see the faint vapour of each discharge slowly curling above the bushes. Almost as soon as the sound of it, comes another rending 'bang' in the air above, and a beautiful cloudlet forms itself out of nothing and sends a sudden rush of screeching shrapnel bullets tearing up the dust— just where no one happens to be.

The three great guns in the background are dropping their ponderous missiles all about the flat now. The air is full of their rushing flight. One of them has discovered a Horse Battery as it comes out from the river across the flat behind us. It is galloping 'for all it is worth, ' and the great shells drop closer and closer each time, seeming to cover it with dust, but not to check it.

That Battery Commander knows what he is about. The Red-Books teach him to bring his guns out in a clump, affording thereby an excellent target for Long Tom, instead of sneaking them one by one into position. But he zig-zags this way and that, to left and right, across the plain, dodging, as it were, the range of the big fellows in the Berg.

Bang! —sudden, quick—in the rank ahead of you, right at a horse's head!

In the flash and roar of the bursting shell, you see the stricken man throw out his arms. As the horse rears backward he comes to the ground clear of him, and lies spread-eagled with limbs outstretched, and blackened, bleeding face staring dumbly into the smiling heavens.

God! —it was sudden. His brother is beside him, lifting a white, horror-stricken face, as he holds the battered head upon his knees.

"Come on, you fellows; never mind that man, " cries the troop-leader, trotting back to where you pause like a crowd at a street accident. You ride slowly past the dead man. It makes you feel bad inside, but wild to rush the fifteen-pounder on the second ridge which did the work.

Now, from its left, comes a sound you had been expecting. Pom-pom-pom-pompom-pom-pom-pom—like an even succession of heavy strokes upon a drum. Horridly screaming past, the little devils go ripping through the lines of horsemen, knocking the dust up all about, but doing no damage—crack-crack-crack-crackcrack-crack-crack-crack!

As the ridge draws closer the din becomes terrific. The great cannon by the Berg boom out their solemn notes unceasingly, and their terrible missiles keep on dropping all about the plain, throwing up huge red spouts of dust and dirt like miniature volcanoes in eruption. From a closer range five or six lighter pieces of artillery shell the ground energetically to our left, as the greater part of the troops on the plain edge that way. There is a continual screaming, rushing noise that fills all the sky. The day shakes and trembles with the Titanic crashing sounds. All the devils of hell are loose about the world.

Tommy Cornstalk

As we halt below the ridge the Berg sends a messenger to the left extremity of the rocks. It lands where they join the alluvial. Such heaps of flying stones and clods of earth spin up from where it strikes as to make you feel that the kopje is in danger of falling down.

The pom-pom in front is turning its attention to the right now, where a regiment of Canadians are stretching at a gallop to seize the flank of the ridge we occupy. The fifteen-pounder sends a message to us to quit, but it flies overhead low down and bursts behind the horses. This little gun means to give some trouble.

Dismounted, with carbines—we are crouching in the rocks and grass, spread out all along the ridge. The plain stretches grassy and fair before us to where that horrid gun works just beyond our reach. Its almost invisible haze shows faintly among the bushes. Another shell comes and bursts in the air lower down—a hundred yards too short—and tears the ground with shrapnel. We seem to be in for a warm time of it if we stay here. Another shot, and they will have our range accurately, and will pepper us.

But suddenly the quick, loud crack of cordite seems to burst in our very ears. Something roars overhead. A little tuft of smoke lifts above the opposite ridge some way beyond the Boer gun. Our own batteries are coming into action behind. We are between two fires. Long Tom howls over us at the battery, the battery spits at the fifteen-pounder within its reach. They lose no time.

Our vis-à-vis bursts a shell in the rocks, and a flying stone breaks a man's arm. Quickly again comes the smack of the cordite—and again, and again, in rapid succession.

There is a rushing wind above our heads, a diminishing roar as they cross the flat, and the three shells seem to land right on the Boer gun. He does not speak any more—at least, not from that position.

Heavens above! but it is good to hear the bark of our own little guns. They are little and light, but there are none in all the world so well served as those of the R. H.A. They snap and snarl at the great baying Long Tom just as a terrier baits a mastiff, and they work in under his far-reaching fire, and discomfort his gunners with shrapnel in the most impudent way conceivable.

The battery behind continues to shell the ridge over our heads for a little time longer. They search it with 'shrapnel, ' and knock the rocks about with 'common, ' and generally seem to inflict discomfort on its occupants. We seem to be the focus of all the sounds of war.

The battery draws all the fire from Long Tom. The shells seem to burst between the guns. They set fire to the grass. The battery limbers-up, and presently opens for a new place. A squadron of mounted infantry comes out of the river and rides back and forward to draw Long Tom's attention from the battery as it changes ground.

Great columns of smoke veil the hills behind as the fires amongst the grass spread rapidly, leaving black patches upon the veldt.

CHAPTER VIII - THE BATTLE (CONTINUED)

All the fight is upon our left hand now. The great cannon of the Berg send their plunging missiles into the soft veldt soil where no one is. They seem to be making gravel-pits.

Assuredly, we are shelved for the day in these rocks. The Brigades are over there, trying to edge round the enemy's right flank; but they are getting a warm reception. Since the fifteen-pounder has become silent our end of the ridge has remained unmolested.

Not so on the right. Ther is a rolling crash of rifle-fire, and there had been the horrid barking of the Boer pom-pom, half a mile from us. The Canadians are being wiped off the face of the kopje, apparently.

But only 'apparently'. In reality, the 'boys' are skilfully 'verneuking' those past masters of 'verneukery'—the Johannesburg Police. We did not hear of it until several nights afterward, but it was very neat.

Opposite the end of the ridge where the Canadians were a large commando of Boers occupied a closer-sweeping spur of 'Fifteen-pounder Ridge, ' well within rifle range. For an hour or more both sides had steadily exchanged shots. The Boers had brought up a pom-pom, and for a time, until silenced by a section of a Horse Battery which had crept up unseen from the river, had worried the Canadians over-much. It was evident that the Boers greatly coveted the position of the latter, and meant to have it if such were possible.

Then the O. C. Canadians did a clever thing. Suddenly calling upon his men to retire, and causing them to mount their horses behind the kopje—the while they cursed him fervently for a coward below their breaths—he galloped his regiment along the rear of the ridge, so that they passed between a gap in it and a smaller elevation behind, and must have seemed to the Boers to be in full and hurried retreat. Once past the gap, he wheeled them quickly behind the little isolated hill that faced it, and waited there ten minutes. A single remaining subaltern watched with his field-glasses from the rocks whence they had come.

Five, six, seven, ten minutes—the Boers kept up a hailing fire upon the ridge, to which there was no reply. They had seen the Canadians stand up to retire, and then ride past the gap, and by now must have felt that the desired position was theirs for the taking. So out they came into the open—a wildly galloping mob of several hundred horsemen. From behind a boulder the sub. waved his pocket-handkerchief.

Now was the chance of the 'darned ol' Colonel'. Back they went at a gallop to the kopje. The lieutenant upon its top was signalling frantically from his rock. The racing Boers were half across the open.

Up through the rocks swarmed the eager regiment. Below the crest they halted, and, following the example of their commander and his officers, stole forward cautiously on hands and knees to the edge that overlooked the plain. Great boulders, and grass, and bushes shielded them from sight. They spread about the top, and laid their cartridges out in convenient heaps, and adjusted sights and elbow-rests. They were to do the thing in style this time.

On and on swept the excited Boers. Oh! but it must have been grand to see the Zarps—the tricky, slim, patrol-getting Zarps, to whom we all owed so much that we wished to repay—riding witlessly into Gehenna. No one fired a shot at them—the Colonel was to judge how close they should come. Nothing was to be done but keep on fixing the sights as the range altered and decreased. It would be a little Bunker's Hill.

At five hundred yards the noise of the thundering hoofs was plain and loud. At four, they were racing for who should be first into the coveted position whence might be raked the whole ridge. It must have been exciting for the Canadians.

On—on—on to three hundred. A fine man on a grey pony led the van, his great beard flowing back against his chest. Now and then he waved his rifle overhead and yelled. It was the Dutch equivalent to a cavalry charge.

Two hundred yards away and they still galloped. The murderous blue barrels of the Lee-Metfords poked out amongst the rocks. Keen eyes were glancing along the steady barrels. Strong hands held men's lives in the twitching of dirty forefingers.

A rifle cracked from the middle of the kopje, and the black-bearded leader left his saddle with startling sudden limpness, and was merely a bleeding heap of clothing in the grass.

Then—what a hell it must have been amongst the Boers; such a hell as they had so often loosed on us, such a hell as must have been at Magersfontein, and amongst the guns at Colenso. For all its length the kopje cracked out smokeless, flameless death. Half a dozen saddles emptied themselves, and as many horses kicked, crippled, in the grass.

On they came still, for twenty yards or so, and many more fell ere they had all turned and were racing back for their lives, leaving a wake of dead and wounded behind them as they fled. Five, six, seven, eight hundred yards, and the little spirts of dust still splashed between the reeling horses. A thousand—and two rounds of shrapnel caught them up and hastened their scurry into the rocks and bushes. Back from the shelter of the bushes came a patter of bullets amongst the Canadians.

The two British guns behind plentifully scattered favours amongst the rocks whither the discomfited Boers had betaken themselves, and presently their fire died away. Forty of them were killed and wounded and made prisoners. Truly, the 'slim' Zarp had met a 'slimmer' than himself!

Without pause the great guns had boomed all through the forenoon, and at mid-day the air still trembled with their vibration. We knew nothing of what was going on elsewhere.

A shining, dancing shimmer of mirage hid the veldt to the left. A great voice came from the placid lake, and where the Creusot shells dropped into its glittering bosom dust and gravel splashed up instead of water. Our own guns were barking from the mirage, but although they may have done good work in silencing the cannon of smaller calibre which were shelling from a closer range they could not approach Long Tom. It was cruelly galling to have to receive all his remarks, without having any chance of joining in the argument.

Nevertheless, the work of the Royal Horse Artillery, as always, was the most excellent thing about the day's operations. Often and often whole batteries sneaked in under the long range of the big fellow— zig-zagging to and fro, literally dodging the heavy projectiles he pelted at them—and burst their little shrapnel in the air above, so that the Dutch gunners found it all too hot about the breeches, and more expedient for the time being to rest under cover at a distance. But whilst one was temporarily out of action, the others would concentrate their fire, and by sheer weight of metal compel the withdrawal of the plucky twelve-pounders and their intrepid gunners.

And here it may not be amiss to remark, that of all branches of the Imperial army none struck the amateur soldier as being so worthy of praise and appreciation as the Royal Artillery. On the whole, the 'regulars' were a disappointment. It seemed to most of us that the army lacked in every essential that was to be effective in such wars as the present, save one or two. It was brave—that went without saying and as a matter of course. It was well drilled—but what did all its training count for here; or what will it count for in the future? It had found 'Brown Bess' very useful in the past; it had done much with the muzzle-loading rifle. Earlier still, it had distinguished itself with spears and bows and arrows. It had used swords with much effect in the days when ranges were numbered, both for cannon and small arms, by the lower hundreds, instead of thousands, of yards. And it clung to the tradition of the smooth-bore and the sabre, even whilst it used the breech-loading gun and the magazine rifle. Because it had found volleys effective against, say, ten thousand men who covered a front of five hundred yards and had a depth in formation of not very many more, it clung to them affectionately in cases where five hundred men extended over a front of ten thousand yards, and had no depth at all. And it made many kinds of a fool of itself on many separate occasions simply by its slavish adherence to systems that nowadays are effective nowhere but on the melodramatic stage.

But the gunners—they were good, good beyond all question or doubt. They, too, had their ancient drill to hamper their mobility and movement. They, too, had the traditions that bands playing into action represent. The heavy harness, the useless kit, the blundering methods of transport were theirs as much as the Cavalry's and Infantry's. But they knew how to use their weapons, and no amount of discouragement ever affected their effectiveness. To silence a British gun you must kill its gunners; even to interfere with the carrying out of its work in any degree at all you must, at the very least, wound half its crew. The Artillery were brave, cool, self-sacrificing, level-headed, disciplined, devoted—altogether admirable. The last word sums them up in toto—they were 'admirable'. Only—their guns might have been better.

Of the Field Artillery we, of French's Division, were unable to judge. One had only heard the booming of their distant guns; but, if they be but one-half so efficient, brave and skilful as their brethren of the Royal Horse, they must come near to being the second 'crack' corps of the British army.

Noon passed. There was nothing to eat. The horses had had the bundles of hay, which they 'wolfed' ravenously, but we had only a couple of holes in our belts—a diet which is by no means sustaining. The guns and pom-poms dinned as loudly as ever, and, occasionally, there was a faint, fierce crackle of rifle-fire far on the left. The mirage had faded away by one o'clock.

Two o'clock—and we lay sleeping in the warm sunlight upon the ridge. Officers strolled about chatting to one another, and looking through glasses at the distant bodies of troops manoeuvring in the haze-enveloped veldt. Below the ridge, the worn horses dozed dejectedly. We seemed to have become mere spectators in the 'Theatre of War'.

But, at half-past three, there came a diversion. In the rising plain that lay between our position and the opposite ledge of rocks was a shallow spruit—a mere depression. It led out from the hills, and lost itself in the veldt. The rocks and scrub where the Boers had had their troublesome fifteen-pounder earlier in the day were beyond our rifle-range. It was the same series of little hills from which the Johannesburg Police had made their fatal raid, but, at our end, was much much further away than where it faced the Canadians. We knew that we were safe from rifle-fire delivered from the rocks, but the depression in the veldt had not been reckoned with.

A lengthy trooper sat smoking on a rock. For the time being he had ceased to be a trooper with a regimental number. He had become a general—and a very 'swagger' general too. From time to time he removed the pipe from his lips, and made caustic comment on the British army and the leaders thereof. Six feet two, straight-backed, broad-shouldered, bronzed and long of limb—sitting there in the sunlight, he struck one as a picture of youthful grace and masculine beauty of form and figure impossible to match. A stubbly growth of beard clouded his strong jaw. The dark shadow of the helmet-peak lay across his eyes and brow in a sharp, black line. His carbine was beside him on the rock. One felt almost proud that the Western Plains could produce so perfect a specimen of glowing manhood.

Perched up there against the sky-line, he was a goodly thing to look at. And some Dutch sharpshooter found him an equally goodly thing to shoot at from the spruit.

He said—what he said does not matter. It had no possible reference to the scenery, or himself, or any other person on earth. But the way he said it made it mean a great deal.

There was a furrow cut across his shoulders from left to right. His jacket was ruined, and his back grooved with a scar, which will only fade as he decomposes finally.

"Damned inconvenient, " he remarked as an after-thought. No doubt it was.

The Mausers rumbled in the spruit—the Mauser bullets cracked and splashed about the rocks where we were and whined plaintively in the air.

It was startling—but we knew the range of the spruit, and although the best that we could see was an occasional crouching figure or a peeping head, and the distance was a good thousand yards, we set to to make it too warm for them to lie in. They had themselves similar intentions as to our kopje.

Everybody lay now behind the most convenient rock. From the whole three squadrons a crackling din of cordite ripped amongst the stones. The two English squadrons fired precise and admirable volleys. The Cornstalk one fired as its individual members thought fit. The so-called 'explosive' bullets cracked like little whips, as they struck near by where you lay.

It is a weird, blood-chilling sound when you hear it for the first time—the whistling of those little deaths in the still air. Not exactly a whistle is it either—something between that and a whir-r, but very business-like and brisk. At first you think that every second of time will be your last upon earth. A bullet flicks your ear, and you make up your mind to take the next one as bravely as may be, and fully expect it to come quickly. Death—sudden, and sure, and bloody— seems inevitable, and, in your heart of hearts, you are afraid— terribly, wofully, loathsomely afraid.

But Death passes overhead, or spits in the dust beside you; and by-and-bye you become familiar with him, and find out that he is not such a bad fellow at all—not nearly so keen on getting you as you had imagined him to be. And you become a fatalist—a mere unthinking fatalist. If you are to 'stop one, ' one will be stopped by your body. If you are to come out scatheless you will do so. In the meantime, your life will be much pleasanter if you don't worry over your chances.

This is a kind of courage. You know that there is danger in those whining voices. You quite realise that the next moment may be your last; but a little custom causes you to regard it all philosophically, and, although to most men being under fire is never a pleasant matter, it becomes an in no wise serious one.

Some there are who have never known what fear is—but they are creatures deficient in nervous organisation, who lack a primary instinct, and who, not knowing what it is to be slavishly afraid, can never rise to the height of overcoming themselves, and doing their duty in spite of the most awful trial to which the mind of man may be subjected whilst he holds his reason.

The cracking bullets continue to smite the rocks viciously. The air still hums with those that pass by. Far down the line you see, as you load, two Englishmen carrying away a limp comrade by his head and heels. No one seems to be 'stopping one' in your vicinity.

But for the pointed rifles and the noise there is nothing visible to indicate a fight—that is to say, nothing that you might photograph. The flying splashes of dust alone show where the enemy's bullets are hitting. Each time you fire there is only a very blue haze in front of your rifle-barrel—so faint that you cannot see it before the rifle of the next man to you.

Over the rocks behind come sweating men carrying a Maxim in their arms. One has the gun itself, another the tripod, others the grey boxes of belted ammunition. A clean-shaven youth directs them.

They pass through the firing-line, and go half-way down the front of the little ridge. Here they set up their pretty toy as coolly as though they were merely a party of surveyors erecting a theodolite to run a line. Some one adjusts a belt of cartridges.

The bullets spit all round them and in between the legs of the tripod and the feet of the sergeant who is laying the gun. The languid officer walks up and down behind, holding a pair of field-glasses, a lighted cigarette between his lips, and issuing quiet orders in a voice indicative rather of boredom than of anything else.

Tat-tat-tat-tat! —all in one breath, but each discharge distinct and clear, and of a note exactly similar to the one preceding it—the sergeant tries a 'sighter'. The lieutenant raises his glasses.

The Boers must be lying low along the edge of the depression nearest us to fire. It is not deep enough to shelter them as they walk about.

"Try nine hundred, " says the officer.

Tat-tat-tat-tat-tat-tat-tat-tat! —obediently replies the Maxim.

"Too short; make it a thousand. " Tat-tat-tat-tat-tat-tat-tat-tat-tat-tat-tat-tat—into one long volume of speedy firing, the little gun raps out its stream of bullets—four hundred to the minute. The empty cartridge-cases, flying from the breech in a continuous stream too swift to see, tinkle on the ground ceaselessly. The belt empties itself—the spitting tube ceases its energetic babble for a moment or two, as a new belt is fitted on; then begins again. The sergeant sweeps the barrel about, pauses, tries new ranges—handles the gun as one who knows its every whim. He is a fine cool man that sergeant, and a very handsome one. Under the hailing nickel he sits and works that invaluable weapon deliberately, steadily, competently. He is the very centre of a little dust-storm raised by the pelting bullets. The Boers are making a target of the gun. Yet he is never scratched. One of the detachment is shot through the chest as he bends over a box of cartridge-belts. He sits in the grass, coughing out his lungs.

There is something brisk and inspiriting about the cheerful tapping of a Maxim in action. It has the air of one who says, "Keep it going, lads. Keep it going—we're knocking spots out of them! "

The edge of the depression from which the Boers had opened fire must have been a 'warm' spot under that pouring torrent of bullets, both from the machine gun and the carbines of the three squadrons. Under their combined influence the Boer fire slackened and died away gradually, a few lone whistles in the air, long after the main body must have evacuated the spruit, telling of the few brave men who were the last to leave—the Commandant and Field Cornets probably, staying behind after the men had refused to face it longer, to fire a parting shot or two at the hated English, in bitterness of soul and disappointment. It must be a hard thing for a gallant man, ready to sacrifice his own life—nominally commanding troops who have such liberty to use their own discretion as the Boer armies had—to contain his soul in comfort when his men refuse to carry out his orders.

We are left in peace again. The damage with us is slight—one man's coat ripped, and one man with a bullet through his forearm—but down the ridge one can see a doctor hurrying from heap to heap, and a few limp forms being carried down to the foot of the ridge. Their position was more exposed and less adapted to taking cover than was ours. Also, they probably did not possess quite such an aptitude for 'taking cover' as the Cornstalks.

The man of the Maxim detachment who was wounded ten minutes ago is dead. He lies face downward in the grass, with his head resting on his folded arms and one leg crossed over the other—just as though asleep. Some one rolls him over to feel his heart. His eyes are half closed, and he is smiling through a hideous slobber of blood about the mouth. In his chest is a tiny hole, but in his back—a gaping, spongy rent. The kind of wound the soft-nose makes.

They buried him presently behind the ridge; and the ground was so hard that they could only dig the grave eighteen inches deep. So they had to pile stones above him. A friend belonging to the gun detachment had laconically remarked: "Puir old Jock—he wasna' a bad bloke". That was his obituary; and, if you come to think of it, you and I will not have done so badly if some one can say that of us when our time has come.

It was four o'clock now, and the sun was getting low. The silly convoy was crossing the river behind us, and coming over the plain after the Division. That is just the senseless way of convoys—they never know that there are any shells to be drawn until one lands in an ammunition-waggon. It is very amusing to see a convoy getting shelled. We watched anxiously from the ridge in expectation of some entertainment.

The fighting was all very far to the left front now. The Division seemed to have been trying to sneak round the right flank of the Boer position all day. At one time, by pushing the Horse Batteries up under the fire of Long Tom, they had succeeded in silencing one of the great bullies; but the other two had spoken with such good effect that the batteries had been compelled to withdraw to a safer distance, and our friend of the tufting smoke, who had been also temporarily withdrawn, came back again and sang his song as merrily as ever.

It was an extraordinary sight that we beheld from our ridge late in the afternoon. The main part of the three brigades were massed upon a slope—or seeming to be massed—three miles away. In front of them, and hopelessly outranged, were the little 'twelve-pounders, ' vainly replying to the big guns of the Boers. All the time the huge shells were dropping amongst our fellows, throwing up great spouting splashes of red dust plainly visible from where we stood. The far away boom of the cannon was ceaseless, regular, ominous. And it seemed to us that the slaughter in the Division must be awful. But it was not so. All the afternoon—we learned next day—they had had but two men killed and some twenty wounded.

Ah! Long Tom had espied the convoy. The shell burst close beside the line of waggons. The column of transport halted as if undecided what to do or how to do it. Another great burst seemed to tear up the veldt, even in the midst of all the crowded waggons. From our far-off position we could hear demoniac yells and screaming of the Kaffir drivers and the volleying creaking of their whips.

Another explosion just beyond the line. All seemed to be in a hopeless confusion, but at last we could see that the teams were turning about and beginning to literally race back over the way they had come. Of course it was all they could do.

But, vividly as one might realise how very unpleasant a thing it must be to drive a waggon with those howling hundred-pounders dropping all about, one could not help laughing at the way in which the Kaffirs bestirred themselves to reach a safer position. The long string of carts and waggons had come crawling up from the river, as though protesting against being dragged along until so late an hour in the day—the very slowness of their march seeming to say, "See how tired we are! " Now, their teams galloped. It was a scurry back to safety. They had barely come within the range of the big gun when he opened on them, but the first half-mile of their retirement was as a chariot race.

Right up to dark the Division clung to its uncomfortable position. The cannon on the Berg boomed without pause. As the red sun went down behind the purple hills, and the short twilight merged into darkness, the flashes of their guns and ours were distinct and clear, and the quick flame of the bursting shells looked like a mammoth firework display. Shrapnel crashing in the darkness has a very fine effect. You see the flash of the gun, sudden and quick, as it is fired; then, as the 'boom-m' comes to you, the shell explodes in the black sky like a great cracker flung high aloft. A pom-pom winks as a signal-lamp, and the little shells striking on the ground are a series of sharp bursts of light.

At dusk the two Cavalry Brigades retired across the river. One by one the great guns ceased to fire. Last of all to stop work was the energetic pom-pom.

Hutton's Brigade stayed to hold the position. We rode back—tired, dejected, hungry—unable to comprehend it all, and believing, though none liked to say it, that we had at last sustained a reverse.

However, it was not a reverse. We did not know until next day that we had simply been keeping Louis Botha and his guns employed whilst Lord Roberts came to Elandsfontein and threatened Johannesburg.

In the camp that night no one was noticeably cheerful. But there was an issue of bully-beef and biscuits, and to men who had fasted and worked hard for more than thirty hours on end, these delicacies were more acceptable than would have been the finest dishes gourmand ever dreamed upon.

So we lay down to rest—battle-stained, weary and unreflective. The cold night closed over the camps by river and Berg. The blessed sleep and rest came welcomely alike to Boer, and Briton, and Tommy Cornstalk.

All the following morning, when we had returned to our places, we drew their steady artillery-fire; but at noon came Ian Hamilton with many men and, best sight of all, his two great 'cow-guns'—six-inch naval giants drawn by thirty-two bullocks apiece, and having another thirty-two to each timber. Four rounds from them and Long

Tom was silently employed in getting himself down to the threatened railway, as were also his brethren of the other positions.

CHAPTER IX - THE HOSPITAL

So much has been said, so much written in magazines and newspapers upon the hospital arrangements in South Africa during the war that one may well hesitate before venturing to criticise, or even to speak of one's experiences in, the Military Hospitals. Members of the Commons have risen up and made statements, to which Generals and heads of departments have made quite opposite statements in reply. Civilians and Soldiers, Society Women and Clergymen, have all argued so much, in this way and in that, upon the good and bad points of the whole Army Medical organisation, that a mere Cornstalk Tommy may well ask pardon for diffidence in approaching a subject upon which the fierce glare of public criticism has, on the whole, shone so adversely. It is a cowardly thing 'to kick a man when he is down'. And nothing in the world has ever been so 'down' in the public estimation as the medical arrangements in South Africa.

In all matters where sins of omission may be charged to the defaulters' sheet of the powers that be, there will always be found ready listeners to any tale of wrong. If you throw enough mud some of it is sure to stick. If you wish to advertise yourself, there is no better or safer way of doing so than by attacking somebody who may not hit back.

One would like best to have written of life in the hospitals as a new experience, as a state of being with which one's readers are not familiar. Life in an hospital ward would present as varied and picturesque sides as in the bivouac and battle. The strange wounds, the queer diseases, the grisly deaths—would all go to form a narrative as interesting, as many-sided, as harrowing or ennobling as the most vividly recounted tale of march and fight. There are stories of as great a heroism amongst the men and women who wrestled with the fierce pestilence of Bloemfontein, Kroonstad and Pretoria, and who laid down their worn-out lives in the disgusting atmosphere of lazarette surroundings, as there are of those who died in open veldt from bullet and shell. There are stories, too, of as great wickedness, as bad and evil affairs as one may ever shudder to hear. Whispered tales, many of them, that you hear as you walk about the lines of marquee tents, in the ships coming home, in divers places where you meet the men who know and have no object in lying. There is good to be told, and evil to be told. There is much that, for the credit of all concerned, should know the light, and very much that, for utter shame of telling, should never in all the after time be spoken.

There is a temptation to air one's views, to grow prolix regarding the manner in which men should have been tended—to suggest, to point out, to dabble in matters which none but professional men may properly comprehend. It is 'cheap' and easy to criticise; it is difficult to have sympathy with a popularly abused state of affairs—to extenuate, to excuse. One desires, of course, to speak without bias or ill-feeling and to suggest, from experience of the actual working of the system, how it may be improved. But the lay ignorance of cause and effect, of undoubted difficulties in transport and supply, and of the circumstances generally, together with the wanton and ignorant manner in which the law has been laid down by all and sundry compel one, in simple fairness to those who may be responsible, to refrain from all but the most deliberate and well-advised statement.

One would, for instance, have the pleasant feeling of doing a public service were one to propose in print that the Royal Army Medical Corps should be better paid than it is. One might point out that the ranking of doctors according to military usage is a pernicious and ill-advised system. It would be delightful to demonstrate that the scum of England are not the class from which tender and devoted nurses of fever patients can be reasonably expected to be drawn. It would be gratifying to show that the equipment of the Peninsular period should give place to that of the finde-siècle, state-aided establishment; that amputations and liver pills are not the justifiable curealls that army doctors might be supposed to consider them to be in all surgical and medical cases. In short, it would be the easiest thing in the world to publish one's own humble opinion as to the good and the bad, the right and the wrong, the wisdom and the foolishness in the organisation, equipment and management of Field, Stationary and Base Hospitals.

But—and this is a very important 'but, ' which it might have been wise of certain M. P.'s, critical civilians, and correspondents to remember—is it quite fair to do so? Is it right and just to set down an opinion at all about anything, until one knows well and intimately all the details concerning the case under discussion? Is it proper for a mere 'casual' to criticise the work—in all its shortcomings and many excellencies—of a system which men of great professional experience and large knowledge have built up in years of practical hard work? One remembers too well that awful period of waiting at Bloemfontein whilst the army rotted inactive, and the little cemetery under the old fort filled and overflowed; when officer, and comrade, and inferior went down alike before the sickle of that grim reaper — Enteric. There is too sad a memory of the delirious, dying men who babbled, in the close wards, of far-off places where there were peace and love. There is no forgetting the carts that rumbled through the streets loaded with those stiff, blanket-shrouded shapes which had been vigorous men—the dwindling squadrons, the crowded sick-tents, the unfed, unwashed, unhappy men who filled them, will never cease to linger in one's memory. And, if one thinks of all these things, one may be bitter, too, against a system which, rightly or wrongly, has had much of the responsibility of them laid at its door.

So, all things considered, it is not well to write as one would perhaps have done unthinkingly, to venture too emphatic opinions as to men and methods, lest one do unwitting injustice to those to whom all the credit they can claim will not come amiss. Wherefore, the writer proposes to merely recount some of his own personal experiences as a patient in various military hospitals between Pretoria and the Cape, and to leave the reader of these pages to form his own opinion as to the right and wrong, the folly and the wisdom of it all.

We were nine miles from Pretoria when it happened—almost north-east. The Brigade was hurriedly saddling-up in the cold darkness before the dawn of a July day. The carts were being loaded. Some one had sent the writer to the top of one of them to assist in the stowing of oat-sacks and biscuit-boxes. The work finished, an eight feet jump from the top had been rashly negotiated. There had been a little stone, that rolled beneath one's foot upon the ground. And the little stone was responsible for a damaged ankle that prevented one from walking, and pained enough for two broken legs. And then, because orders were hurried and imperative, the squadron had ridden away and left one lying upon one's kit in the open veldt.

The long and the short of it was that there was no ambulance van to carry us into Pretoria. Beside the writer there were two sick men of his own corps and some twenty of the three English regiments that made up the Brigade. An old 'spider'—a four-wheeled waggonette, commandeered from some farm—had been left behind, and, with a couple of debilitated mules as motive power, the various kits and possessions of the dismounted men who remained were to be carried into Pretoria on it. Kindly arms lifted the writer to the top of the piled-up baggage, and by dint of prodding with naked swords, butts of carbines, and other impromptu goads the worn out animals were induced to commence their unsteady trek into the Transvaal capital.

But the rolled kits fell off at intervals, the waggonette jolted mercilessly, and the ride was so comfortless and painful that, after half a mile had been traversed and the roadside that led into town from Kamiel Drift reached, we were constrained to beg our conductors to leave us there, on the faint chance of being conveyed into Pretoria by some Army Service waggon going in to get supplies for the troops that held the hills by Derdepoort. And so we were left lying on the grass—and there seemed to be every likelihood of our staying there indefinitely.

The red road stretched out to the gap in the hills where the infantry camp was, and, in the other direction, round the end of an intermediate ridge, to Pretoria. Men came by on horseback and in Cape carts, and there was one on a bicycle; but that day the Army Service Corps seemed to be resting. The sun went up into the deep blue, and the beautiful day grew older by two hours. Specklike on the sky-line one could see the black dots of pickets who were watching Louis Botha from the hills.

From seven until eleven we lay by the roadside, and no good Samaritan passed by. Once there came a mule-cart with a Kaffir driving, and one of the two who were able to walk begged him for a ride into Pretoria and the hospitals.

"Nie, baas, " he replied; "mule too tire. No can carry some more. "

"You black beast! " remarked his interlocutor; "you black swine! —if I felt a bit stronger I'd commandeer your dam team and make you walk! "

Nevertheless, the Kaffir was quite in the right. The welfare of his team should have been, and was, his first consideration. He merely smiled, and passed on.

It grew to be dreary waiting for what might never come. Had we had any rations and not been ill and crippled, to stay there would not have troubled us overmuch, but as it was—far from water, one of us seeming to sicken for fever, another hardly able to walk, and the third quite incapable of standing and whose only means of locomotion lay in what he could do by hopping, the outlook was alarming and miserable enough.

But at length, in a cloud of red dust, there came a slate-coloured empty waggon along the road. A brick-faced sergeant with a flaxen beard sat upon the box beside the black driver. Languidly the prospective enteric case shuffled into the road, and took up a position in such a place that the team of mules must either run over him or stop. They stopped.

"Now then, laad, " said the sergeant, "what for be ye blockin' t' road? Doan't y' know we be in a dom hurry t' git some bre'd from P'toria? Stan' a won soide—there's a good laad! "

Wearily our envoy explained the situation.

"Who be ye? " asked the sergeant.

"'Stralian Horse, " said the sick man.

"Oa, aye—ye be t' Orsetrailyans, be ye? Well, kom along, laads. Rackon there's room f' ye, if ye kom from Orsetrailyer. Me brother Dick went there. Whaat! —can't th' laad walk? Bide a bit, naow, an' I'll gie ye a han'. "

So, finally, we came into the Market Square—shaken and tired and sick with pain—and were left upon the pavement by the new hospital in the Law Courts. We lay upon our kits on the red tiles, and contemplated the Dutch Church, and the pedestal that had been built to hold Paul Kruger, and the magnificent Raadzaal with the gilt angel soaring from its roof, and the flapping Union Jack mocking it in the breeze. And it seemed that we might lie there also indefinitely. No one came to ask us whom we might be or why we sat there waiting. Generals and Tommies,

Colonels and Burghers walked past and hardly looked at us. There was no room for sick men in the world of war.

They had put a square of galvanised iron fencing about the front of the Law Courts, between the high steps and the Church.

"I think we'll go in there, " suggested the man with the headache; "we might have more of a show to get to bed if we go in there. "

So we went in and squatted upon the lowest step, and an orderly came and looked at us, and went away into a corner to smoke. The thought came to one: "And there was a certain beggar named Lazarus... moreover, the dogs came and licked his sores".

The clock in the Raadzaal front marked the quarter, half, three-quarters—and no one came. Just before the hour was reached a medical officer strolled out on to the terrace above and surveyed us. "What are you men doing theah? " he queried, shaking a surgical knife at us; "why don't you come to attention? "

He of the aching head and stomachic pains climbed up the steps. He seemed to be trying his best to stand to attention, but it was a dismal failure, to say the most of it. The nonchalant surgeon conversed with him awhile, and the two of them came down to us.

"Er—you men, " he said, "you men, you know, you ought to have gone to a Field Hospital. Why didn't you go to a Field Hospital? What? Can't possibly take you in heah unless they send you from a Field Hospital, you know. 'Gainst all rules. Quite irregular, you know. What? No, we can't possibly admit you. Beds all full, you know. Quite out of the question! "

"We don't want beds, sir. Can't we come in and camp on the floor? We're used to sleeping on the ground. "

"Oh, deah, no! We don't do that kind of thing heah, you know. Don't know what you had better do, I'm suah. Don't ask me. Can't you go to the Rest Camp? " And he strolled inside. We felt that we were the scum of the earth. But our turn was to come.

A man came riding through the iron gate on a fine bay horse, and instantly the orderly sprang to attend him. He alighted as one who knows all about a saddle, and handed the bridle reins to the obsequious 'Tommy'. It seemed to us that there never could have been so soldierly or so fine a man to look at. 'Gentleman, ' too, was written all over him. He was a tall, dark-complexioned man—well-preserved, and somewhere between fifty and sixty. A black moustache and a tuft of hair upon his chin, after the manner of Lord Roberts, gave him a somewhat foreign aspect. He wore the flat, German-pattern staff-cap of khaki with the red band round it, and the red lapels upon the collar of his tunic that indicated staff rank. As he ran actively up the steps into the hospital he glanced curiously and keenly at us, half-paused, and went on inside. We must have been a picturesque trio enough to turn the gaze of any man who had not a soul enmeshed in red tape. The sick man was gaunt, unshaven, hollow-eyed and pale; the man with the blistered feet was slim, larrikin-like and alert; the writer was minus boot, and spur, and puttee, as regarded his right extremity, and dirtier and more unkempt than he had ever thought he would become. We had been out getting shelled all the day before—on a big reconnaissance—and had come in late, so that there was no chance of washing or shaving before the morning's daylight start. Therefore, it was nearly three days since we had used soap and water.

Twenty minutes, and the handsome staff-colonel was striding down the stone steps. As he came to the bottom one on which we sat forlornly he stopped, and spoke: —

"Well men, what is your trouble? Why don't you go inside? Wounded, eh? " "No, sir; twisted ankle—can't walk. "

"And you? "

"I feel very sick, sir. Headache—weak. "

"And you? "

"Skin orf one foot, sir. Can't walk or ride. Blood-pois'nin', I think. "

"Well, why don't you go in and get attended to? Who are you? "

We told him that we were Australians, and that we had sought admission unsuccessfully, and had not the least idea now as to what we should do.

"Oh, you're Australians, are you? Well, your fellows have done some good work. Stop here. I'll go and see what can be done. " And he went up the steps two at a time.

To be an Australian seemed to be something of a distinction here. But it is curiously true that no matter with whom, if you said you were an Australian you had a much easier time and got what you wanted more readily than before it was known from whence you hailed. Perhaps they made allowance for our ignorance.

Down he came again, followed by three anxious-looking medical officers, chief amongst whom was the tired individual who had been unable to give us room.

"Now, " said that angel in disguise, "now why are these men left here? "

"We really have no room for more, sir. The waggons are still at Nitral's Nek, and we expect another convoy in to-night. It is quite impossible to take them in. "

"Well, what are you going to do about it? "

"I really do not see how the matter affects us, sir. "

"Do you not? Ah! —well, sir, it should affect you! And it will affect you. Do you think it a very creditable thing to your Hospital that these men should have been sitting here for nearly two hours without food or water or any apparent chance of ever obtaining any? Do you not consider that, since you have become aware of the case, you would have done rightly if you had passed them on to another Hospital where there might be room for them? I think that you have been very remiss in your duty, sir.

"Now will you kindly write a note to the P. M.O. of some other Hospital where you think they may be taken in—explaining the case to him. Where do you think they would be likely to find room? "

The man who disliked irregularity seemed to have become quite contrite by this time. Evidently the Staff Officer was a great gun, since all stood so much in awe of him.

"I think they might get into the Racecourse Hospital, sir. They can expand their quarters there—plenty of sheds and buildings, you know. We cannot here. " "Well—give them the note. "

He strode out of the enclosure, and presently reappeared with a cab.

"Jump in, men, " he said. "Up to the Racecourse, driver. You'll be all right now, eh? "—and he was on to his horse and gone almost before we could thank him.

It is unlikely that that officer will ever see these pages. We never heard his name, nor did we meet him again, but if he be alive and should chance to drop across this book and does not forget the incident, he will know that three sick Cornstalks were very, very grateful to him for his kindness that morning by the Law Courts. His courteous care for the welfare of three dirty vagabonds is one of those things which only the Recording Angel books to a man's credit. He was in this, and doubtless always, following in the steps of his great leader, and ours—the soldier's warmest friend—Lord Roberts.

So down Church Street, past Paul Kruger's lion-fronted dwelling, past his beloved Dopper Church with the unfinished clock in the steeple, up towards the railway, across some open ground, and we came to the Racecourse, which, having been in the early war time a prison, was now an hospital.

It was a good course—one could see that with half an eye—but it made a wofully bad hospital.

Here, also, it seemed that we exhibited the usual bad taste in not applying for admission in the regular and pre-ordained form. A fat sergeant-major of the R. A.M. C. was for turning us away again—which would have been awkward, seeing that we had dismissed the cab. But the embryo enteric flared into righteous wrath; wished to know whether we were luridly qualified stray dogs, or what; claimed personal friendship with the P. M.O., and demanded that he should be shown where that officer abided, so that he might himself present our letter of introduction.

Such a queer place for sick men to go in—such a quaint, unconventional, singular kind of hospital—you never saw! What the conditions of life were in the grand stand, or the saddling paddock, or in the big pavilion where the luncheons might have been, none of us could say. We lived in loose-boxes in the stables—and to this day one of us pricks up his ears when he hears corn rattle in a box, or beholds horses feeding out of bins. It was a long galvanised-iron shed. There was a passage down the middle, with a door at either end, presumably for ventilation. Sick Kaffirs dwelt in the passage, and rendered both night and day hideous with their chatter. Widely projecting eaves made a kind of verandah all round the building. The doors of each stall were in two halves, after the kind of stable-doors. In front they looked out across the level ground about which lay the course, and in rear on to a tidy garden shaded by gum and wattle. We were assigned quarters in the front.

Many days we lived there, not getting overmuch attention medically, but still living — which was something. If you had good luck you obtained a bag or two to spread out ere you laid your blankets on the ground. This was the ward where slight wounds, rheumatisms, sprains, mild dysenterics, and ripening enterics 'most did congregate'. Here, also, were the malingerers. It was astonishing, and rather appalling, to note the number of hale beings who lived in hospital. Sad and humiliating as it must seem, any man who has been through the Military Hospitals can quite easily testify to the truth of this. 'Fed up' often seemed to be about to assume just as alarming proportions as enteric. How they did it was a mystery. One can only assume that, in many cases, the medical officers, though morally certain that a man might be shamming, were too disgusted to take the necessary steps towards 'bowling him out'. And, indeed, dealing with the typical 'old soldier, ' hardly any measures in the world, severely preventive or otherwise, would keep him out of hospital were he desirous of staying in. If a man steadily persist in having a pain in his chest, and be fairly consistent in his symptoms, you cannot, without very great difficulty, prove him a liar. And as the doctors had always very much more to do than time to do it in, they could not afford the almost detective-like vigilance necessary to properly meet the cases of such wily characters.

A résumé of the day's doings in our stable may perhaps give the reader some idea of what life in this most rudimentary of hospitals was like. It is well to bear in mind, however, that these were the first months of the British occupation of Pretoria, that De Wet was blowing up the railway every day on the other side of the Vaal, that fever and dysentery were rife in all the camps about the town, and that it was utterly impossible to obtain many of the most essential supplies required by an hospital. When you come to consider these points it is wonderful what the Medical Staff did even so primitively well as they did.

Soon after daylight a bugler sounded the 'reveille' — most beautiful, if most unwelcome of 'calls'. Half an hour later an aggressive individual walked hurriedly along the stable front, and rattled a stick against the corrugated-iron doors. If that did not bring your slumbers to an end nothing would do so. If you could stand, or hop, you arose and opened the doors of your compartment, and yawned in the fresh air. There was a pump by the side of the track whereat you might perform your toilet. You folded up your blankets, and tidied the den as well as might be. Then came another orderly with a basket full of cut loaves of bread. You received a piece, supposed to weigh one pound, which was to last you all day. Sometimes he threw it at you—and on those occasions you were not quite certain as to whether your habitation were a loose-box or a kennel. Humourists used sometimes to request to be supplied with a bran mash, complaining pathetically that they felt 'a bit out of condition'.

At half-past seven buckets of tea arrived in the open before the sheds. Cripples, and ill, and shams hobbled, and slouched, and rushed with empty beeftins, mess-cans, jam-pots—anything that would hold water. Eating and drinking utensils were not supplied in that part of the hospital. You somehow got some tea and ate some bread. Every second day a pot of jam was served out to each four men. After breakfast the stalls were still further tidied, the pots polished and hung up on the wooden partitions, and the front of the shed swept and garnished.

And at 9 a. m. there came the P. M.O. —the Great Finality of the establishment. At the Racecourse he was a very popular person—a man with a face that you might trust, the quiet air of one who knew his task, and the kindly sympathy of a good physician, even yet unspoiled by the years of narrowing army service. Everybody liked the Major—we did not hear his name—and he seemed to like every one. In spite of the fact that his hospital was probably as rough and primitive as any you might come to in all Africa, the mere fact of there being so likeable a man at the head of it atoned for very much in which it fell grievously short of perfection. One can still think with affection of the man—his grave, clean-cut, kindly face, with the iron-grey, close-cropped hair about the temples; the slightly stooping figure and the pleasant laugh. And the remembrance of his quiet courtesy of speech, and the close attention with which he listened to what you had to say is a gleam of sunshine over a retrospective outlook that is dreary, and sordid, and commonplace enough. He was cruelly handicapped by want of the most necessary things in carrying out his work, but no one left that disreputable place who had not, at least, a good word for the Major.

At noon the buckets brought soup with raggy meat in it. There was milk for those who were nominally on 'milk diet, ' but as everything was much in common the patients ate, as a rule, what they considered best suited to their tastes, diseases, or constitutions. All the afternoon was a long 'loaf'. You slept, or read, or wrote letters home, and at 4.30 came more tea, with which you finished the remainder of the bread and jam.

Night came—and you smoked, and yarned, and went to bed in the dust. And byand-bye, when the long-winded ones had ceased to talk in dialects, and brogues, and twangs, and all—even the vociferous Kaffirs—were asleep and still, rats ran about over your head, and nibbled your hair.

Ten days of this, and the writer was one morning, with some thirty others, conveyed in ambulance-vans to the Pretoria railway station, and started off in a bullet-marked carriage to Cape Town, with five days' rations of bread, and bully-beef, and jam. At least, we thought we were being sent to Cape Town—but when you start upon a journey at one end of a military railway which runs through an only partially subjugated hostile territory, you do not really know whether it will be a week, or a month, or a year, or all eternity before you reach your journey's end. This time the journey took two months.

CHAPTER X - THE HOSPITAL (CONTINUED)

THE train ran through the hills between two of the silent forts, which had cost so much money and had been of so little use to their builders, and out from the valley of Pretoria into the open veldt. The track of the invading army still lay beside the line. The traffic of the convoys had worn the grass away, and the road was mile-stoned by the parched hides and whitened bones of horses, mules, and oxen, and, less frequently, by the red-mounded, final resting-places of men. Many had remained to 'settle on the land, ' but the tenure of their occupation was probably more permanent and abiding than most of the poor fellows had expected it to be.

Past the little wayside stations of Kaalfontein, Zuurfontein, and various other fonteins—and about three o'clock we arrived at Elandsfontein, the junction of the Cape and Natal lines to Pretoria and of the short six-mile one which ran into Johannesburg.

The train waited ten minutes, twenty minutes—an hour. Coffee was brought to us in the carriages—drunk—the bucket taken away again by a Kaffir, and still we moved not—no one knowing why.

At length we went on. Somehow it seemed to us all wrong. We should have been rolling across the open veldt again, but we were instead passing through the suburbs of a great city, and every moment the houses grew larger and denser. It was like coming into Melbourne in the afternoon—except for the tall smoke-stacks of occasional mines, and the stampers, and the big cyanide vats. Past little suburban stations—as 'Zimmer and Jack' and Jeppestown—in through gardens, and trees, and pretty suburban streets, along a cutting and below a bridge, and we ran in under a high domed roof of glass, and came to a standstill beside one of the platforms of a great railway station, much larger and finer than Redfern, or Flinders Street, or the North Terrace.

It was Park Station—and then we remembered having seen it before, when the illustrated papers made pictures of the refugees crowding into open trucks, in the mad rush of September to get away. And we remembered another picture of a commando going to the Front, and wondered vaguely where all those bandoliered and booted warriors were now. They were in graves, and at Simon's Bay and St. Helena, and in the veldt still; and we held their towns and railway systems—

but had we finished yet? How long was it to be before those silent streets of the outskirts should fill again, before this great station should hum with the busy life of the resurrected city, before the black smoke lifted above the chimneys of the mines, and the great town should have recovered from the paralysis of war?

As we waited there we heard the wherefore of our waiting. The line had again been blown up, just beyond the Vaal. Popular rumour credited Christian De Wet with the deed, and probably rumour, for once, was right. Most of us had a sneaking regard for De Wet, and looked upon him as a great, though sometimes inconvenient man— but this afternoon upon that train he was exceedingly unpopular.

By-and-bye they shunted us into a siding, and commanded us to 'get out, ' and so we alighted as well as we could, and sat upon our kits beside the carriages and trucks. As dusk settled down over the town, ambulance-waggons came and carried us away to the Amblers' Club, where was located Number 'K General Hospital. There they put us into bell-tents, pitched on the football-ground—four in a tent—and they fed us on bovril and bread, and we slept upon stretchers, which was the nearest approach we had made to sleeping in beds for nearly a year, and was a decided improvement upon the litter and dust of our late quarters in the horse-stalls. It was dark when we arrived, and beyond the fact that great buildings within high trees and park-like grounds loomed vaguely in the blackness, and the faint white showing of many marquees and bell-tents glimmered obscurely about us, we could make little of our situation and environment.

Next morning was beautifully cold, and clear, and fresh. No wind stirred the tops of the tall blue gums that, hedge-like, surrounded all the enclosure. The buildings of the Club stood up amidst them, picturesque in their setting of green leaves. Part was unfinished, with the scaffold poles and ladders still erected about its raw and new-looking brick walls. There had been a fire before the war, and the outbreak of hostilities had left the work of restoration incomplete.

The tents we occupied were pitched upon a grassless square of recreation ground. Tiers of wooden seats surrounded the enclosure. Below it was another square, and, in the front of the building, an excellent cycling track and cricket ground, and still more excellent tennis courts. The great concert hall of the Club was used as a ward for the more serious cases. It contained beds with real sheets and real pillows. They struck one as being useless, unnecessary adjuncts of an effete civilisation, after so many months of doing without them. Even the loose-boxes at Pretoria had seemed at first to be commodious residences. It is only afterwards that you look back and shudder. Comfort is a matter of comparison. To the sick soldier lying in the veldt on a wet night a hollow log, or the lee of a paling fence, would seem the very acme of luxury. But when you get to civilisation again the reputation of necessary insecticide will hopelessly damn an hotel in your estimation, and you will quite easily turn up your nose at food for which, in bivouac or on outpost, you would have bartered your last 'fill' of tobacco.

On the whole, the hospital in the Amblers' Club was an improvement upon that of the Pretorian Racecourse. In the first place, the condition and location of the buildings and grounds were in every way suitable for an hospital. Centrally situated as to the city, not fifty yards from the principal railway station, amply large in its grounds for the exercising of convalescent patients, surrounded on all sides by wide streets, and with a high galvanised-iron fence having but two main entrances—both from the points of view of its administration and of its patients no site or arrangements could possibly have been better adapted for the successful treatment of sick and wounded and the maintenance of necessary discipline than were those of the one in question.

We were more comfortable in the little tents, though it was strange how full four stretchers and their occupants made them seem, even after the usual dozen or fifteen human beings who smothered in them in the ordinary standing camps. The food, although practically the same as supplied to us at the Racecourse, was better cooked and better served, but in this bracing climate of cold, clear, winter weather, to men whose naturally fine appetites were in no wise impaired by their physical injuries, the ration scale was wofully insufficient.

A very excellent thing was the fact that for the most part the hospital, or at least the division of it in which we were, was served by orderlies of the St. John's Ambulance Association.

There is no branch of the Imperial Army so generally unpopular with all other branches as the Royal Army Medical Corps. This is a large, loose statement apparently, but it is unfortunately none the less perfectly true. Were one to account for it by stories heard in and out of the hospital one might possibly be merely repeating calumnious untruths, but there is much, apart from hearsay, that one has seen oneself, and which all Colonial soldiers have seen also, to render fairly evident Tommy Atkins' dislike as a class to the privates and non-commissioned officers of the corps. He seems to regard the men of the R. A.M. C. as being essentially on a lower plane than himself. He has bestowed upon them contemptuously the appellations of 'Poultice Wallopers, ' 'Linseed Lancers, ' and other insulting and more ribald designations too Atkinesque to mention. As a primary reason for having incurred Tommy's bitter dislike it may be that the rank and file of the R. A.M. C., being technically non-combatants, are unreasonably looked down upon by men who are. And, when he 'goes sick, ' Tommy has to do just what he is told by these despised beings—which is, doubtless, very galling to Tommy. "So, " says he, "w'en we meets the swine artside, we breaks their bleedin' 'eads. If they sees yer comin' darn the street, w'y they bloomin' well dodges hup a halley. "

Personally, one is almost ready to excuse many of the shortcomings of the much-abused orderlies, by consideration of the fact that you cannot expect the services of a perfect being when you pay him something that comes to a little more than a shilling a day. If a good personnel is required, then it will have to be paid for. And you won't get 'much of a man' to do the kind of work the R. A.M. C. are called upon to do under five.

Now the men of the St. John's Ambulance Association were volunteers and enthusiasts, besides being, in ordinary life, men of a very much higher social grade than the class from which the private regular soldier is usually drawn. They therefore took more interest in their work than did the men of the R. A.M. C. They may not, perhaps, have been quite so well trained and disciplined, but they were certainly kinder, gentler, and more sympathetic in their treatment of patients than were the regular orderlies. And so they incurred Tommy's gratitude and esteem—since Tommy is a gentleman who is nothing if not just in his estimate of superiors and equals.

The routine is much the same as at the Racecourse. 'Reveille' sounds early, and presently there comes the ward-master, usually a sergeant, to turn you out. Blankets are folded, and stacked neatly at the head of each stretcher. The walls of the tent are rolled up, and its interior and immediate vicinity swept and cleaned, after breakfast has been served, so that the resultant crumbs may not meet the eye of the visiting medical officer. In the meantime, if you are physically capable of so doing, you go for a wash.

Now here is the worst one has to say of this otherwise—considering the circumstances and the times—exceptionally well-regulated and administered establishment. At one end of the main building of the Club stood a long wooden trough, raised some three feet above the ground on trestles. Each morning it was filled with water from a stand-pipe, and in it scores of men performed their ablutions. One may imagine that the water became fairly 'thick' after a little time each morning. Well, that did not matter so much. You cease to be over-particular as to small details of this nature after you have learned what it is to go seven days without any kind of 'wash' at all.

This was the thing that mattered—sufficient care was not taken by the authorities to isolate cases of infection or contagion, so that the unrestricted use of this common washing-place might—and in one instance known to the writer actually did—endanger the health of all the inmates of the hospital.

But—to return to our routine. Breakfast over, and the lines garnished as aforesaid, the medical officer in charge of the ward to which you belong goes his rounds. His advent to each tent is heralded by the sergeant poking his head through the canvas door-flap and thunderously yelling, "Shunmedcalorfcer! "—which use has accustomed you to translate as "Attention! Medical Officer". So you turn out, and stand with your diet-sheet—a mysterious document whereby you obtain varieties of the scanty rations that are going—one of a row before the tent. You must stand there, even if it be only on one leg and a stick. The sergeant snatches the sheet from your hand, the swift physician glances keenly at you out of the corner of his eye as he initials it, does the same for your three companions, and hurriedly passes on to the next tent, where already the war-cry of his satellite has preceded him.

The inspection over, there remains naught to do but smoke, if you have tobacco; read, if you possess any literature; sleep, if you think you can, or otherwise put in the time until the bugle sounds the dinner-call. Dinner consists of the same boiled cubes of leathery meat floating in thick soup and a few potatoes in their jackets, served up in the little enamelled-tin basins in which you draw your morning and evening tea.

The long afternoon passes monotonously. The best that you may do to while away the hours is to sit still in your own or another tent, and listen to the bloody and hair-raising accounts of side-lights of the war. Many of them, though couched in simple and profane language, and not for publication, are true and real beyond question—a great many of them are untruly and gloriously sensational enough for the 'copy' of the most unveracious correspondent of the average London Daily Shocker.

There was a Cornstalk who came to a marquee in which certain of us were sitting one rainy afternoon. Most of those present were Englishmen and Canadians. One little group of four or five sat in a dark corner, and smoked silently—content for the most part to listen to the stirring tales to which, we felt, we could never hope to approach in interest of adventure and startling detail. Our compatriot was a member of a certain famous Australian corps, which had distinguished itself all through the Western Campaign. It would be unjust to him to say that he was boastful. He was not. He merely told his tale in a dignified and simple manner that took it straight to the hearts of his listeners.

The writer had not the good fortune to share in French's dash to Kimberley. He knows no more about it than what he has been told by men who were there, and what he has since read in the newspapers, and magazines, and books. But he is quite sure that he will never in all his life read such a graphic, nerve-stirring, sympathetic narration of that great cavalry march as he heard from the guileless lips of his gifted fellow-countryman that winter afternoon in the dark interior of the fourth marquee, of the second row, in the upper football-ground of the Amblers' Club Hospital at Johannesburg.

It was not merely immense; it was 'epic'. He told us of the gathering of the host at Ramdam; of the organisation; of the setting forth; of the fighting near Klip Drift; of the miles of waterless veldt beyond the Modder. In harrowing manner he recounted the sufferings the men had endured, the awful thirst that killed horses by the hundred, the running fight. Clearly and lucidly he made plain to us the magnificent generalship of Johnny French. We could not but suppose that, in rare occult fashion, the plans of that 'deep' customer had been evident to him from the very beginning of the operations, and that for our benefit—there, right there in that humble place—he was letting us peep along the quiet backways where the unseen elements of history walk darkly.

We felt elated and triumphant that we—we dozen or so of common soldiery—should learn these things, first-hand and hot, from one who knew. It would be something to talk of through all our uninteresting after-lives. It was a dreadful march, it was a wonderful march, it was the military movement of the ages; it was a soul-stirring and ennobling recital, such as we had never looked to hear from mortal lips. Kinglake might have approached it in stately minuteness, Archibald Forbes or Steevens could not have come near it. What a pity, we thought, that he had not lived before, so that he might have been with Caesar in Gaul, or with Napoleon from Moscow or across the Alps into Italy!

As though we saw it all, we rode with him into the shell-battered Diamond City. He showed all the happiness and sadness of the welcome of the lately besieged. We saw the Kaffirs ravenously swooping upon the entrails of the worn-out horses shot at the completion of the march, little white-faced children, and the anaemic women, coming from the mine-shafts. We saw and heard Cecil Rhodes; beheld the wonderful gun Labram the American had built in the De Beers workshops. He took us to the scarred trenches, the littered Boer redoubts and gun emplacements; and next morning we went out with him to rout the remaining Boers by Dronfield. Bill Adams at Waterloo was as a Policeman at a Botany 'push' fight compared to this hero.

And when he stopped, and went away to get tea, a man of his own corps, who had gaped with us, unseen, from the darkness of that corner in the marquee, could only gasp brokenly, "Wonderful, wonderful! Oh, dam wonderful! "

And that expressed the feelings of us all.

"Yes, " continued his comrade, "it's the wonderfullest yarn I've ever heard. Why—the blarsted liar! —we went to Kimberley in Febroory, an' he didn't leave Sydney until April! "

None the less, it was the finest story ever told—and although it was sadly true that the narrator had never been to Kimberley in his life, had never seen the Modder (save at the Glen, north of Bloemfontein), had never been under fire during the war, and was 'a consistent and shameless pom-pom dodger' all his days—he was gifted with an imagination and power of expression that Virgil or Dante might have coveted. One had the inclination, but not the power, to run after him, as he strolled modestly away, in order to grasp him by the hand and say, "My brother, you are the most gifted and accomplished liar that Australia ever produced! " And, when you come to think of it, that would be saying a great deal.

At night they gave us candles, and we lay upon our stretchers, smoking and reading, until the time came to 'turn in'; or wondering whether we were to stay for ever in Johannesburg, and what the town might be like; or speculating as to how they must be thinking soon of shearing out at home in Australia. Everything seemed very quiet out in the soldier-ridden city. One could make out, beyond the top of the lower fence and through the straight stems of the bordering eucalypti, the bright globes of incandescent light that shone over the empty streets. Later, there came the far, faint challenges of the sentries about the Market Square—and once, about midnight, we heard a rifle-shot, and a scream of pain, and, turning over drowsily, wondered what the poor devil had done.

There was a week of this—each day exactly a reproduction of the one before it, no evening that differed from the last—and then one mid-day, in the sudden fashion by which things are carried on on active service, the writer was warned amongst others to be ready for the train at one o'clock, in order to start again for Cape Town.

Of the journey down one need not speak at length, although it was the most exciting train journey the writer has ever taken. There was never any chance of being bored for lack of interest in those days between Pretoria and Kroonstadt. Every culvert and bridge over which we passed seemed to have been blown up, at least once. The engine that drew our train was bullet-marked about the cab and boiler; the closed trucks in which we travelled nearly all had little round holes somewhere through their walls. The first night we stayed at Vereeniging, just beside the Vaal, and waited there until morning.

When we had crossed the river, and come to Viljoen's Drift upon the southern side, news came that the line had been again interrupted further down. It was noon before we recommenced our journey, and by the next evening we had not come to Honing Spruit. We had passed the Kopjes Siding where De Wet had nearly caught Lord Kitchener in person; and Roodeval where he had unmistakably caught the Fourth Derbyshires, and had blotted out everything of the station save one shell-torn iron tank and a steel safe, and where the mails and winter clothing lay half-burned over acres of veldt.

Honing Spruit was but eighteen miles from Kroonstad, but no train ever travelled in the darkness over that part of the new colony. So we waited beside the little entrenched station, and about eight o'clock were turned out of the trucks into the trenches to assist in repelling an expected Boer attack, which, however, never came off.

At Honing Spruit there was a quaint but doubtful story of a stray Canadian, who, somehow, was somewhere along the line with various other details in a little entrenched post, guarding communications. It was his duty to ride out each morning along a length of line, in order to find out whether all was clear for the trains to proceed. One morning, having sallied forth as usual, at some distance out he espied five industrious beings busily employed in levering up a rail. They were so intent upon the work in hand that they did not perceive their avenging Nemesis, and he was able to approach them within two hundred yards of the scene of their exertions, still unnoticed. At first, he thought of riding back and reporting his discovery in the orthodox way, but being a Canadian, and therefore dowered with a delightful freedom from all the restraining trammels of Red-Book rules, he decided 'to score off his own bat'. So he dismounted, tied his horse to a telegraph-pole, rested his rifle over an ant-heap, took careful aim, and shot a Boer. As the startled men sprang to their feet in astonishment he shot another, and, whilst they were hurriedly seeking to mount their horses, he 'bagged' a third. The remaining two escaped.

The Canadian strolled over to the three bodies, and found each one of them quite dead. Doubting whether his comrades at the post would believe his unsupported story of having singly engaged five Boers, killing three, and putting the other two to flight, he—what do you think? —he took their scalps!

We reached Kroonstad for breakfast, remained there until nearly noon, and arrived at Brandfort in the evening. On the railway bridge near the latter town, a sentry had recently been 'sniped' by some enterprising sportsman, from the bed of the river, on a moonlight night. Accordingly, nowadays, the more representative burghers of Brandfort paraded with the guard on the bridge, and took turns of 'sentry-go' in military overcoats. There had been no more 'sniping'.

Bloemfontein we came to in the 'wee sma' hours of the next day, and were immediately taken from our trucks, given a drink of hot milk and bovril, and placed in the bell-tents of the big canvas hospital under the long kopje where were mounted the Naval guns, and which since the British occupation has been known as Naval Hill. And next day, as a further stage of our progress to the coast, we were drafted off in batches to the various hospitals about the town and its vicinity.

One has written at greater length of hospital experiences than at first intended, but, as they would be incomplete without some account of the five weary weeks at Bloemfontein, we shall speak of the great hospital in the veldt, westward of the town, whither we were sent, in another chapter.

Moreover, the writer had opportunity of seeing, as it were, the Military Hospitals in three very representative stages. First there were the primitive arrangements, typical of the extreme Front, at Pretoria, where you slept in stables and fed like pigs. Then came the Amblers' Club, which was a sort of intermediate stage between inferiority and tolerability. Thirdly, we come to Number 'N' General, at Bloemfontein, which, at the time when we were inmates of it, was a good type of the Stationary Hospital, so located that every necessary thing might easily be procured; and which, therefore, had to stand or fall in one's estimation upon its own merits, and could shelter behind no excuse of interrupted communication—for then, and for many months, the lines to Port Elizabeth and Cape Town were both open to traffic, and supplies were coming through regularly, and in sufficiently large quantities to meet all requirements.

CHAPTER XI - THE HOSPITAL (CONTINUED)

Number 'N' General Hospital stood to the west of Bloemfontein, on the rising veldt that stretched away to Kimberley. You came out past the white-columned Raadzaal, through the bushes that fringed the outskirts of the town, kept northward of the great clump of willow trees that had been so cool and shady when we came before—but were bare and leafless now—crossed a deep spruit, and arrived at the wide-spreading city of snowy canvas. On the higher skyline were redoubts and trenches, infantry and artillery camps, and, standing up clean and sharply-cut against the bluest of all blue skies, the gloriously purple, far-off peaks of conical and sugar-loaf kopjes— miles, and miles, and ever so many miles away through the clear, dry, closer-bringing atmosphere.

And if you stood, ere you entered the lines and streets of gleaming tents—stood just on the threshold of the suburbs of that strangely-peopled city—and looked back across the intervening veldt, your eye took in a picture of such sunlit beauty, such clear and smiling sweetness of earth, and sky, and distant glowing hills, as you will never in all your 'afterwards' remember but with pleasure and delight.

Across a mile or more of bare, brown veldt the buildings of brick, and stone, and iron nestled in their beds of evergreen eucalyptus and leafless oak and elm. Spires, and walls, and gleaming iron roofs studded the deep-green and gold-grey beauty of their lovely setting. The dome above the Raadzaal, the steeple of the Dutch Church, the floating Union Jack over the Presidency, lingered in one's vision beside the rest. At one end the old fort rose above the clustering roofs on its little kopje, at the other there stretched away from us to eastward the long, flat bulk of Naval Hill. Away behind, forty miles away, yet clear and sharply showing in every curve of outline, lay blue Thaba N'chu—the great historic mountain of the brave old Voortrekkers. Down to southward, in the rolling ridges, were the little groups of shining distant tents that marked the outposts in the wide perimeter of possible defence. Between them and us, beside the road that had led in the march from Driefontein, was the great Rest Camp—a bewildering massing together of bell-tents.

If you have gazed long enough across the open to beautiful Bloemfontein, and have drunk in all the loveliness of scene we used to sit and watch through many afternoons for hours unweariedly, it will be worth your while to turn and look at what is close to you — the trim orderliness, and clean regularity, and manifest respectability of Number 'N'.

It is a wonderful place, a kind of new world of weird beings in bright new clothes, and spurred and booted surgeons who never rode a horse — and, above all, it is the kingdom of 'Mad Jack'.

There were streets and lanes of stately marquee tents — one great group upon the right hand, and another upon the left, and, in between, an open space with galvanised-iron huts for stores, and kitchens, and washing-places. In the background there were acres of bell-tents — tenantless now, but once upon a time (which the orderlies speak of yet shudderingly as 'the fever time') full to overflowing.

Each marquee is dressed in its line, correct and level to the quarter of an inch. Every guy-rope is uniform and symmetrical with regard to every other, every peg is driven into the ground at the same angle as every other peg, and all are whitewashed. Along each broad highway are whitened stones, set evenly in rows upon the ground, and, at the corners, little heaps of boulders, also of a glowing whiteness.

There is nothing here that stands out from its surroundings. All is uniformity and monotony of sameness. The patients are dressed with an exact similarity — blue flannel trousers, ill-fitting flannel jackets of the same vivid hue, red neckties, and yellow slippers; and each man blows his nose upon a red cotton handkerchief with a white border. The orderlies are all in khaki serge, the officers in uniform, with puttees or leggings, and sometimes spurs. The Nursing Sisters glide from tent to tent, in their neat grey gowns with the red capes about their shoulders, and white muslin headdress — pleasant to behold, and generally pleasant to speak to and be nursed by, and always, one thinks, good, brave gentlewomen.

In our marquee there were five Tommies and the writer. There was a private of the West Riding who had been a colour-sergeant — but was 'smashed' — suffering from rheumatism, and so bad that he was unable to bear the coldness of sheets upon his bed. Next to him, one of the Scots Guards, badly wounded in the groin. Then a Fourteenth Hussar, who said his heart was weak. It was — but not in the way he sought to impress the doctor with. Beside him lay a little lance-corporal of the Essex Regiment, whose trouble was synovitis of the right knee. Opposite the writer's bed was that of a broken-jawed private of the Oxfordshire Light Infantry. The writer was the only un-English resident, and, being an Australian, was a person of some consequence in the community.

Comparatively all the appointments of the marquee were on a scale of unexampled luxury. There was a tarpaulin on the earthen floor by way of carpet. We slept on beds—real iron beds with spring mattresses and sheets—think of it—sheets! There were counterpanes, too, and pillows with pillow-cases, and they were changed as soon as ever they began to get dirty; and we had night-shirts, and day shirts, and all manner of fine things. There were little bedside tables for each man, and there was a bigger table by the door of the tent with a looking-glass on it, and plates, and knives and forks, and enamelled bowls to drink from. And we had an orderly to attend on us—(only he didn't, he got us to attend on him)—and we were quite suddenly become as millionnaires and princes, who have everything they want and a good deal they don't want—which we had too.

But a bed—a real bed—just think of it! You may laugh if you like, you who read this enthusiastic boastfulness of beds, but just you sleep upon the bare ground under the stars, wet and dry, every night for seven months, and when you get into a bed again—a real, soft, comfortable bed—you will never want to leave it. The good Captain B——, who visited ours and two other marquees, felt the writer's ankle, and put it into plaster-of-Paris, and sent him to bed for three weeks, and the writer knew himself that, if it had been for three years, he would have borne it cheerfully. My goodness! but it was fine. The luxury of it!

And so, for those restful weeks one was in bed, and there were opportunities afforded Tommy Cornstalk of studying Tommy Atkins at close quarters, such as he had not had before—and the little Sister, and Mad Jack, and Keen the Orderly, and the Boy Chaplain, who served out funny little prayer-books with swords, and guns, and lances printed on their covers—and all the other variously interesting types of humanity who moved about the hospital.

It was a curiously interesting experience. It would be just as interesting to an inmate of a pauper asylum or a gaol. One found new types of men, of whose existence one had merely read before. There were tales of strange lives and of a different world to the one we knew of in Australia. There was the quaintest profanity in language, the most singular and notable slang to be met with outside the chronicles of Mulvaney and his allies. There were anecdotes of life in barrack-room such as we would not repeat to a Chinaman; there were stories of garrison towns that would shock Beelzebub. Robbery and rape were homely topics amongst those delightful army types. Getting drunk was never such a glorified feat as one heard it spoken of in Number 'N'. One has lived and worked with all manner of outcast men to whom obscenity was wit and blasphemy the salt of conversation, but never has one, or never will again, perhaps, encounter such strange gifts of foul-mouthed loquacity as one lived through in that five weeks at Bloemfontein.

And yet—one never will meet again five kindlier souls, or more generous, or better disposed, or more unselfishly ready to assist a helpless comrade. One may never forget the quiet little helping ways they had, whilst one lay in bed unable to assist oneself. The red-headed Guardsman, who was the foulest souled of all, swept the floor about one's bed in the mornings, or walked painfully to the reading tent and brought back books, out of sheer good-heartedness. The little Dublin guttersnipe who graced the Essex mended one's trousers, and refused so much as half a fig of black tobacco by way of repayment for his trouble. And they were all just as kind and helpful to one another. Sampson, who talked with difficulty by reason of his bandaged jaw, moved silently about the tent doing perpetual little jobs of tidiness. They were the tidiest men in the world. But most soldiers of the regular army are that. Imagine the same class in a shearer's hut!

The day commenced with the arrival of Keen from his quarters. Keen was a Cockney-Scotchman—at least, that is how West Riding described him. He was always desirous of buying things from you, which he would sell to some one else at a higher figure. "Yah! blinded, bloomin' Sheeny—vat you dinks!"—he of the Guards would remark by way of 'riling' him. The Hussar sold him a coloured blanket—the cheap sort you may purchase anywhere for a few shillings, and the design upon which was a most startling combination of all the cardinal colours. Keen traded it to the little Sister as having come from Cronje's laager. The amount of stuff which Cronje must have had stored in that laager was simply enormous. You certainly never buy any Boer curios or relics except upon the understanding that it was salvaged from Paardeberg. It cannot be genuine otherwise.

Shortly after the coming of Keen, a man brings the day's allowance of bread—a very liberal one here. Nobody gets up much before breakfast-time. A bucket of water and basin are the means of toilets. The buckets are beautifully clean and polished in Number 'N'.

One pot of jam was given to us each day, and one ounce of butter for every man. Besides these delicacies there were, as 'extras, ' a tin of cocoa paste, two pineapples, twelve oranges, four bottles of stout, and two ounces of whisky in common amongst the tentful. The broken jaw and the 'rheumatism, ' also, had special diets of their own.

Immediately after breakfast those who were able to move about assisted Keen in sweeping out the tent, making the beds, and generally cleaning and polishing all the plates and utensils in use, so that everything might be neat and 'shipshape' against the coming of the Doctor at ten o'clock. If the weather were fine, the canvas sides of the marquee were looped up all round, so that the air might circulate freely and keep the atmosphere of the tent fresh and sweet.

Just before the advent of the Doctor, the little Sister who had charge of the row of marquees in which ours stood came to see that all was right. If it wasn't she bullied Keen unmercifully. It was almost ludicrous to see the compact little woman, with the firm chin and tender eyes, ordering about great, hulking men who could have carried her in their pockets, so to speak. She always had her way— which, however, is not unusual with her sex. She, too, was Scotch, but her speech was much prettier than Keen's.

When the Doctor came we all lay in, or upon, our beds with our board-mounted diet-sheets in our hands, and he took a lot of cheerful trouble over each of us, and was civil, and witty, and alert— much more alert than the Hussar desirous of heart-disease supposed. Every one liked Captain B— —. He was not a regular R. A.M. C. man, but belonged to some volunteer medical corps in London, and had a good practice privately, Keen said. Keen knew everything.

'Extras' were drawn from the Quartermaster's stores at eleven o'clock, and we drank the drinks immediately—by way of diversion—and kept the fruit until the afternoon. The cocoa paste was made use of after dinner and at night, making a couple of bowls apiece, with hot water from the cookhouse, which Oxfordshire procured by reason of possessing a 'towny' amongst the cooks. We lived well in our marquee, principally owing to the pushing ways of Keen—who levied commission on all he obtained for us—and the kindness of Captain B— —.

Dinner was mainly 'roast varied'—which is meat, gravy, vegetables, salt, mustard and pepper, in a little flat tin. The tins were carried from the cookhouse in a hot-water tray, so that they kept warm.

The afternoon was a time of sleep, of lurid conversation, or reading, or draughts, or chess, or dominoes, or cards. At four o'clock little niggers came through the lines selling the Bloemfontein Post, which we always bought. There was little enough of news in it, and its leaders were obviously inspired, but there was occupation and interest in trying to read the Dutch pages, and any news was better than none. Its telegraphic items relative to the war were probably much more reliable than those of the big papers in England and Australia at the time, but they were usually many days old. The Post was the successor of the Friend, which had been a so bitterly anti-English journal before the British occupation, and a so brilliantly edited news-letter for the few weeks immediately after that event, when it was under the control of the war correspondents.

Tea was at four-thirty, and sleep came about nine o'clock. Every day was as the one described. They never varied to a quarter of an hour. You ate the same thing and did the same thing every day as you had done yesterday and the day before, and, after a week of it, the monotony of existence was unspeakable. One seemed to have become a machine. After the activity of life at the front, the lack of exercise and change was the most trying experience of all the war. At times it affected men's spirits strangely, and one has heard of cases of melancholia arising from the enforced idleness of hospitals coming in so sudden contrast to a mental state that pulsated with interest and excitement.

One must make further mention of 'Mad Jack'. To speak of Number 'N' and pass that worthy over would be as though one told of the sea and ignored the fact that its fundamental element was water. 'Mad Jack' was the fundamental element of Number 'N'. He had the sending of patients to Capetown, and as most men wished to get to Capetown, if only for a change, most men came into contact with him, and most men wished subsequently that they had rather come in contact with the Evil One himself. It was amusing, but disastrous to your chances of a trip down country, to go before 'Mad Jack, ' and let him see what your inclinations were.

He was in charge of a large part of the hospital, and held army rank as a Lieutenant-Colonel, and was a most curious and interesting character. Short, wiry, slightly knock-kneed, with legs very much shorter than his long, flat-backed body, and dressed in a khaki uniform that did not fit him well, and with leggings some sizes too large for his calves, he was a strange figure as he stood outside his office-tent making fiery speech to the luckless patient or orderly who might have chanced to incur his wrath. A keen, square-jawed, sun-tanned face peered at you through gold glasses, as though he sought to probe your very soul with his choleric gaze. Popular report credited him with having been in the Army Medical Service for more years than most of us could count to our ages. He had been previously in Africa in '81, in India, in Malta—in all, or nearly all, the many places where British soldiers go.

But it was of Ireland of which he seemed to wish you always to bear in mind that he was a son. Should it happen that you were Irish also—Cork for preference—then, indeed, was your bed a bed of roses and your path an easy one. They said that he had done good work down about Colesberg in the early year, and that he had been mentioned in despatches for conspicuous gallantry. And they told all manner of stories about him—his sayings became proverbs, his quaint wit and quainter wrath subjects of laughing talk in the marquees at night. No one who has sojourned in Number 'N' can possibly forget 'Mad Jack'.

A civil surgeon, doing duty at the hospital, had, at his own request, sent a certain man before him whom he (the civil surgeon) had recommended for Capetown.

"Phwat ails ye, me man—phwat ails ye, phwat ails ye? Can ye not sphake—what, what, what! "

"You told me to come and see you, sir, and Mr. S——sent me up this morning. " "Shtand up sthraight, ye scoundthrel—shtand up sthraight in y'r boots! I didn't tell ye anything av the sort—what, what, what! "

111

"But, sir, I— —"

"Shtop y'r 'buts, ' me man. I tould ye nothing av the koind. Kape shtill, now! Phwat d'ye mane by comin' here thryin' to tell me I said such nonsinse? I niver said it! "

"Well, Colonel D— —"

"Now phwat d'ye mane by y'r insubordination? I'll get ye two years, me man. Phwat ails ye, I tell ye? For why do ye not answer me? Is it dumb ye are? Come here—come here into the loight, till I look phwat koind av a man ye are, at all. Why don't ye tell me phwat's the matter wid ye? What, what, what! "

"Well, sir, I've had enteric, and the Doc— —"

"Ye've had no such thing at all. Phwat d'ye know about enteric? Who tould ye ye'd had enteric. Ye've not! Ye got a bullet now, didn't ye? What! "

"Yes, sir, but I had enteric after in— —"

"'Twas a bullet, ye Irishman! Phwat soort of an elephint ye must be not to know the difference betwane a gunshot wound an' faver? D'ye want to go to Kep Town? Now shpake the truth, me man. Do-ye-want-to-go-to-Kep-Town? What, what, what! "

"Yes, sir, I'd like— —"

"Well, ye won't! Ye'll not go to Kep Town! Rist Camp, Rist Camp, Rist Camp! Mark him 'Rist Camp, ' sargint. Sure ye're just the bhoyo for th' Rist Camp! " "But, sir, I'm feeling very weak, and— —"

"Wake, is it? Ye fale wake. Ye don't, ye don't, ye know well ye don't! Go along wid ye, me man—isn't it the tickey beer in Kep Town an' the Dutch gurls ye're thinkin' of? What! Look here, me lad, ye were never so well off in yer loife as ye'll be in the Rist Camp. Sure, the Colonel 'll thrate ye loike his own son. Aw, yis, ye'll go to th' Rist Camp. Sure, it's a grand place entirely. Kep Town! —Kep Town! — what, what, what! Now, I'll just tell ye what, me bhoyo—a fortnight in the Rist Camp an' two years in China 'll jist put ye roight. Ye'll be a new man afther it—what, what, what! "

"Oh, damn it! —won't you let me speak? "

"Phwat's that, phwat's that? Who are ye, who are ye? Phwat d'ye mane be comin' here shwearin' an' cur-rsin' loike that? Who are ye, who are ye? Phwat rigimint do ye belong to? "

"Oh, Second New Zealand Contingent. "

"Aw—these dam Colonials! Mark him 'Kep Town, ' sargint—get out, get out o' me soight! Sure, I get no pace at all wid you Austhralians, an' Canad'yan's, an' New Zealanders! Go on—get away off to y'r marquee! Y're not fit t' thravel! Mark him 'further tratement, ' sargint. Alright, alright—go away! Go away—out o'—me soight. Aw, yes, yes, yes! Ye'll go to Kep Town—anywhare t' get rid av ye! "

The above is only a sample of the style and manner of this quaint creature. He strolled about the Camp, stopping and questioning men on all kinds of astonishing subjects. He was, without doubt, the greatest feature of Number 'N'. An encounter with 'Mad Jack' kept you laughing to yourself for twenty-four hours. No one could ever forget him.

But under the quaint, eccentric manner and the quizzical fury of his denunciation there beat a good heart, and he was, in his own way, a kindly, honest gentleman enough. He may have been a singular curiosity, but he was a rough diamond also.

Sometimes, at night, neighbours would drop into your marquee. And there had come one who was a 'bleeder'—at any rate that is what he of the Fourteenth said of him. It seemed to be a pet name for a typical low-class Londoner—a slum-dragger, one of the very much 'submerged tenth'.

There were other Hospitals down the line—there were Wynberg and Woodstock, for example. But has not the voice of the M. P. been raised in the land, and has he not told you all about them from the fulness of his knowledge and vastness of his experience? And when you are told a thing isn't it wise to believe it always—if you want to? There was, too, the wonderfully perfect ambulance train that bore us Capewards, but if you wish to become learned as to ambulance trains read "With Number Three". [1]

[1] Rudyard Kipling.

Personally, after the lapse of months, one has dreary memories of life in hospital; but it was very much better than one had expected it to be.

CHAPTER XII - THE MAN

It was a hot morning in the veldt, somewhere between Abraham's Kraal and Aasvogel Kop, in what was, as yet, the Orange Free State. We cooked a pumpkin beside a ransacked farmhouse, and felt bitterly resentful of the fact that a belted Staff Officer was chasing a fowl in the background with a drawn sword, and were fiendishly delighted when he tripped over an old wheelbarrow, and got his well-fitting khaki clothes lamentably dusty. He saw us laughing, and looked very angry, and then laughed himself and went inside, leaving the hen to whom she might concern. We were too weakly hungry to be concerned about her.

The mirage shone in the valley, and swallowed up a train of transport-waggons slowly lumbering out of the haze behind. Mile after mile the long procession had staggered by, the cries of the Kaffir drivers came shrilly to us through the clear morning, the cracking of their whips sounded like far-off rifle-shots. A low cloud of reddish dust floated into the blue sky beside the line of march, stragglers drifted past on foot and horseback—weary, boot-worn, mulish, patient Tommies, whose rifles seemed to weigh them down; sweating, cursing, disgusted 'flash' colonials leading lame horses; sickly boys belonging to Cape regiments, whose worn-out 'chargers' had given in at last and were dead behind—all the strangely assorted flotsam and jetsam that struggles wearily and perfunctorily to keep pace with an army marching forced marches.

They were hungry days those—when the army left its base by Modder Bridge, and dived suddenly through the enemy's country in a swift dash for his capital. They were exciting, eventful days. Osfontein had been followed by Driefontein; Driefontein was to be sequelled by the siege and surrender of Bloemfontein. The great battle for which we all looked, but which did not come, was still looming in front of us. Each day brought us closer to what, we thought, was to be the bloodiest struggle of the war. When, three mornings after, we left the regiment upon the Cape-Pretoria railway, and, scouting forward in the uncertain dusk of dawn, from the top of a low ridge beheld the pretty town below us, heard the homely crowing of cocks, and saw the peaceful blue smoke ascending from beneath the early morning coffee-pot, we hardly could believe our eyes. The great final struggle, from which we were to emerge conquerors of all South Africa, and which was to bring Paul Kruger suing hastily for peace, had again eluded us—but here, two days before the expected fight, we watched divisions and brigades and guns and teams go past, and cursed fervently the luck that had lamed our horses, and left us, rationless and forlorn, in the tracks of the advance.

My friend was of Roberts' Horse—a full-bearded, tweed-trousered Victorian—for all the world like a Boer, and having nothing soldierly in his make-up, save a worn and faded khaki tunic, a bandolier, a slung rifle, and a straight back. We had foregathered earlier, in a mealie field, and quarrelled over the possession of a pumpkin; but a compromise had established amicable relations, and, at noon, we roasted the heaven-sent vegetable in a fire of shelled mealiecobs, beside that white-washed, abandoned farmhouse.

In the house we had foraged unsuccessfully for food, but everything seemed to have been removed, or destroyed, by its recent tenants. In a barn was a great heap of unthreshed Kaffir corn, but some one had thoughtfully anticipated the coming of hungry rooibaajes by emptying over it a drum of tar.

Upon the stoep without lay an old book—a Dutch Bible, clumsily bound in leather, printed in curious ancient type, and bearing upon its title-page the date sixteen hundred and eighty something in Roman numerals—a veritable treasure and priceless relic for any book lover. In the front was written in faded yellow characters "Gert van somebody, " and a few lines of Scripture. In the back cover was a long list of family names, with dates that ranged from 1690 to the end of the seventeenth century—a kind of genealogical tree. Poor people—their terror-stricken flight had been so hurried and hasty that, though they had taken everything beside, they had left what was probably their most beloved heirloom to the spoiler—the accursed bogey of a rooinek, who might have helped them to load it up also, had they only waited.

The Bible was carried in the writer's haversack for three long hours, and it was large and heavy. Then Providence sent another pumpkin into his path, and, there being but room for either food or Gospel, Gospel had to be left in the veldt, and food transported to the camping-ground in place of it. We were very hungry—but now that that hunger is a memory and not a stern reality, regret has taken its place. You never know what manner of a depraved creature you may become until you are really hungry.

Tommy Cornstalk

As we stood beside our miserable fire eyeing the blackening slices of pumpkin with starving impatience there came another great Staff Officer, trotting hideously, to whom spake the hunter of fowls, emerging from the house. We caught faintly the words "Commander-in-Chief" and "coming, " and in reply—"No; next house—lunch is ready there, " and he of the misshapen riding-trousers trotted back again—a moving eyesore as he bumped upon his uneven way.

And soon after, down from behind the stone cattle-kraal to our left, a group of Staff Officers rode at a walk. Behind them came a body-guard of bearded Cape Colonists and Uitlanders. At their head rode a little old man.

He was just as he looks in the portraits that have overrun all the papers of the last two years, and was quite the kind of man one had expected to behold, except in this one particular—that he was even more diminutive than we had expected him to prove. In the Headquarters Staff there were many big men, and this fact may possibly have emphasised the smallness of his stature, but by himself, or in a crowd, he can never be anything else, so far as physical development goes, than 'little Bobs'.

It was a never-to-be-forgotten morning for the writer—that of the 11th of March, 1900. It was one of those rare times to an Australian when the lump of enthusiasm comes up into your throat, and you can say nothing, and think of nothing, and do nothing—only feel. It seemed impossible to realise that one was really gazing upon one of the idols of one's boyhood, and that, unlike most idols, this one had not proved to have 'feet of clay'. One thought hurriedly and vaguely of the homesick boy going out to join the Bengal Artillery, years and years ago; of the footnote below his own modest telling of the gallant deed that won him the V. C.; of the Siege of Delhi; of the Kashmir Gate; of John Nicholson; of Cabul and Khandahar; of the dead son lying in Natal; of Paardeberg, of Osfontein, of yesterday—of everything about him that could flash through one's mind in half a second.

He barely halted to say a word or two, inaudible to us, to the fowl-hunting Staff Officer, who had mounted his horse and was awaiting the arrival of the Staff before they came—and then he moved on, speaking earnestly to a handsome younger man who rode beside him.

"Who's that crowd? " laconically inquired the Victorian. "Who's the ole feller? " Ignorant swine!

There was little time in which to notice very much before they had come, and passed by, and were out of sight upon the other side of the farmhouse—but one impression, stronger than all others, remains. Of all the Staff he was the freshest and most active-looking by a very great deal. It was not hard to realise that, since the Army had left the camp by Osfontein, it had been a time of great strain and long hours for all of them. The tired, weary figures, sitting their horses stiffly, spoke eloquently enough of the state of being of the Staff as a whole. But the little man at their head rode as a 'flash' shearer who has just 'rung out' a shed—alert, springy, vigorous, and very fit. Excuse the comparison, you who know flash shearers. It merely refers to deportment.

One has written of him above as a 'little old man'. 'Old' he is—one knows it; and 'little'—one has seen it. But he is the youngest old man you might come across in a thousand years. His figure is slim, and straight, and active. The scrupulously neat khaki uniform fitted him as a glove. The puttee leggings encased the trimmest little legs that ever pressed against stirrup-leathers. His brick-red face had been fresh shaven that morning—one would swear. His was the most graceful form you might ever chance to behold, and he carried himself so bravely, and modestly, and handsomely, that one felt as though some old knight had stepped from a bygone century into this, endowed with all the best attributes of the 'age of chivalry'. It came across one's thought that here, indeed, was a man of whom it might be said again—'sans peur et sans reproche'.

He went on, and, full of pumpkin, we, too, went on later in the day; and, in course of time, he led a procession of Guards and other tattered foot soldiers through Bloemfontein, whilst we camped five miles outside, at Wessels' Farm.

The next occasion of the writer seeing the 'great little man' was in the Market Square of Bloemfontein as he walked across on foot towards the Club, attended by the beetle-browed Kitchener, and two less important personages who followed a little way behind.

One could not but comment upon the striking contrast presented by the appearance of the two great soldiers—a contrast which is not only of appearance, but of every deed and the manner of its doing.

They were both great men—one had but to see them to recognise that fact. Even had one never heard of them before it would have been apparent at a glance. But between the stern, relentless, sphinx-like countenance of Kitchener and the kindly humanity that looks from behind the features of Lord Roberts there is a great difference. Only in one characteristic is it possible to compare the two faces— and that is the indefinable something that spells 'success, ' the strong, steady, sure look that speaks most eloquently of great mental power, of unswerving purpose, of a will before which other wills must bend or break.

In physique every one knows how greatly they differ. Kitchener is a big man, even amongst big men; Lord Roberts is a little man amongst little men. But each of them, according to the scale of his construction, is a splendid specimen of vigorous manhood. The one is comparatively young, straight-formed, sure of step, and long of limb; the other is very old for an active General, and short of limb— so short that were Kitchener to walk with his usual stride, 'Bobs, ' one thinks, would need to trot, in order to keep pace. But he is just as straight, just as erect, just as imperiously commanding in his looks. Both of them are men of steel.

In course of conversation with an engine-driver on the railway between Kroonstad and the Transvaal capital, the manner of the two men was strikingly exemplified by his words.

"Oh, yes, " he said, "Bobs an' Kitchener comes along sometimes. My colonial, y' oughter see the difference at the stations, though! W'en 'Bobs's' train pulls up, he gets out an' strolls along the platform, an' everybody knocks off work so's to come up an' have a look at him. He jes' walks about among the crowd, talkin' to 'em like me an' you would. Asks 'em how they're gettin' on for rations, an' so on. 'Course, he's never familiar, or anything like that—y' can always see he's Boss—an' if he notices anything wrong he lets 'em know, quick an' lively—but he seems to be more of a friend to everybody than anything else. But w'en 'Herbert' steps out of his carriage there's hardly a soul to be seen on the platform—they're all away diggin' trenches, or mountin' guns, or scoutin' roun' the country—any blessed thing, so long as he can see 'em workin'. Lord help 'em if they ain't! W'y I b'lieve if Kitchener was to be given command of heaven's gates he'd jes' as soon Stellenbosch Peter, spite of all his long service, supposin' he caught him nappin' any warm afternoon! "

On another afternoon, we had been up Maitland Street to where, it was said, a baker baked bread in a little lane that opened from it. We had found the place, and there had been a clamouring queue of Tommies from all the world, so that it seemed one might wait indefinitely on the 'off' chance of a loaf of hot bread, and the possibly full chance of getting none. So we had come away mourning, and were leisurely walking down the street on the right-hand side as you come towards the Post Office, when we noticed a throng of officers, and tattered privates, and sweating Dutch civilians seeking entrance to the Town House.

"What's on inside? " we asked a military policeman near the door.

"Dunno, " he replied, with the customary ignorance of the British soldier as to what may proceed beneath his nose. "Dunno. Specs it's a meetin' o' they blarsted Christians. "

We went in. Even should they prove to be 'blarsted Christians' we were anxious to see what they were about. It was long since we had sat for an hour beneath the roof of a public hall or place of entertainment. It would be almost refreshing not to feel the blueness of the sky overhead for a little while. And so we entered—there were difficulties about doing so. We had to squeeze in through the throng, heedless of protest; and, finally, we stood against the wall under the gallery of a large hall. At the further end was a stage. In the midst of a setting of scene that might have stood for Dunsinane Wood, or the Forest of Arden, or Eugowra Rocks in Robbery under Arms, was a little table with a water-bottle upon it, and a little man—the Little Man—beside it.

All the hushed audience strained its melting faces towards the stage. There was a greasy smell of perspiring men, of new bread, of tobacco-laden breaths. Clumsy feet sometimes shuffled on the floor. But, though the hall was packed as tightly as it might be with hotly living soldiery, there was a hushed, exciting silence of the kind you only find when there speaks publicly to a great gathering some one whose most trivial word the gathering does not wish to lose, whom it is worth their while to listen to, and who knows what he is talking about.

He was speaking. We stood upon tip-toes to see him, and strained also so that we might not miss any word he said.

Tommy Cornstalk

It was a meeting of the Army Temperance Association—apparently organised by the big-bearded chaplain who sat upon his right hand, and who also subsequently said something that was not interesting—and of which, we learned for the first time that afternoon, Lord Roberts was the President.

He spoke quietly, and distinctly, and to the point—he was like a little Maxim, tapping out its emphatic arguments rapidly, unmistakably. There was nothing of the 'Great-I-am' or the 'this-is-so-because-I-say-it' style of oratory about his speech. It was direct, conclusive, and to the point; and he spoke as one grown man speaks to another. He was not to us, that afternoon, the Commander-in-Chief, telling us what we must do—he was simply our friend 'Bobs' suggesting, in all kindliness, what we should do.

He spoke of the march up the Modder. It seemed that it was a greater one than the march to Khandahar. He enlarged upon the privations the troops had had to endure, the footsoreness, the weariness, the difficulties of Driefontein. He said how sorry he had been when it was wet, and what a fine thing it was that we had been unable to get drunk. (Well, it possibly was a fine thing.)

He said he had never led such an army as ours, and that he very much doubted whether any one else had done so either. We marched well, we fought well, above all we behaved ourselves well. Under the clear-cut eloquence of the little man we almost managed to believe that we were models of good behaviour. We felt glad that he did not seem to have realised how very dearly we would have liked to loot Bloemfontein, how much we would have enjoyed but half a day of the swashbuckling license that other armies had enjoyed in other wars. We felt sneakingly glad that he had such a good opinion of us. We almost realised what 'whited sepulchres' feel like.

But when he went on to enlarge upon the sobriety and steadiness we displayed in the streets of the conquered Free State capital, the absence of crime, and the lack of defaulters, and attributed it all to the temperance principles that actuated the army, we wondered whether, possessing as he did all the elements that go to make a good man, he really lacked in what has been spoken of as the 'saving grace of humour'.

For this was the state of affairs. You went to the Bloemfontein Hotel and demanded beer. "Are y' an orficer? " asked the dissipated ruffian who served the bar. —"No. " "Well, git out quick's yer can. " You went to the Royal Hotel, and the ubiquitous military policeman threatened to run you in. You went to the 'Masonic, ' seeking refreshment, and, though your tongue hung out a yard by reason of your dryness, they ejected you summarily. One recollected these experiences, and felt almost inclined to call loudly from the back of the hall: "Oh, Bobs, go slow! It wasn't our fault that we were temperate—you funny little man. You seem to be pulling our legs! "

None the less, although he seemed to credit the army as a whole with virtues it did not possess, no one who has ever seen war can fail to realise how much wisdom the commander of an army displays when he prohibits the use of intoxicating liquors to his troops upon entering a town. War is terrible and brutal enough when conducted by sober combatants. What it would be when waged to its logical conclusion by drunken fiends one's imagination almost fails to picture.

One could not say that the speech was a triumph of oratory. It was not. There was nothing dramatic in all its length, nothing whatever that might appeal to the emotions. But it was lucid, clear, forcible— and the manner of its delivery was the manner of the man. It may have been as when a schoolmaster jokes, and all the little boys laugh heartily, but, glancing round the hall at times, it struck one as being extraordinary the way in which the 'Tommies' hung on to every word that dropped from beneath the grizzled grey moustache, noted every point of the quick discourse, applauded every telling argument brought forward. And most of them seemed to be telling arguments. Never once was there the slightest sign of the air referred to above as that of the 'it-must-be-right-because-I-say-it' class. The greatest soldier of the Empire was speaking to some of the meanest, yet at no time did he seem to be conscious of their, and his, relative positions. Always, it was as man to man—never as Commander-in-Chief to Tommy Atkins or Tommy Cornstalk, or any other humble 'pillar of the Empire'.

He sat down, and the meeting spent ten minutes cheering him. From what one knows of Atkins it is almost safe to say that there could have been scarcely a score of men amongst the soldier audience who were enthusiastic advocates of temperance. In all he saw of them the writer cannot recall one single instance where the British soldiers were not enthusiastic advocates of beer—plenty of beer, unlimited beer. That is one of 'Tommy's' faults. He will sell his soul for beer. It was not, one grieves to say, that Tommy applauded the manly and wholesome sentiments of the speaker. It was his fanatic love of the man that prompted him to cheer so heartily. One does not sit in a hot building all through an afternoon to hear the kind of thing, good though it be, that one may hear any Sunday afternoon in any park at home. It was to hear the Little Man speak, to listen to his kind voice, to see him, and to look what manner of man he might be, that brought us mostly there.

While he had been speaking one almost fancied that beneath the quiet earnestness of all his words, the clear-cut, hard-hitting sentences, there lurked a vein of sadness, a quiet undertone of grief, which might never come in words to the surface, but which, one still fancied, might nevertheless be there. One thought of the dead son at Colenso, and of the guarded houses, and the lenient proclamations, and the scowling people, and wondered whether there could be many men like this one at our head—who would bear no malice, and evidence no iron hand towards the people who had slain his only son. Of course, he should not have allowed personal feeling to sway his actions in such a manner, but most men would have done so.

Once again, at the Vet River, our Brigade was drawn up on the northern bank, just after crossing, and we were told that the Commander-in-Chief wished to inspect us. We all looked upon it as a privilege, and were eager to have the Little Man ride through our ranks. For we were proud of our Brigade. And then, just as he was coming, the writer and four others of his troop were sent out scouting all the way to Smaldeel. We were infinitely disgusted, but we had to go.

Months afterwards, as we lay encamped one morning beneath the guns of Daspoort Fort without Pretoria—having been hunted thither by De la Rey from Nitral's Nek during the best part of the previous night—some of us had seen him ride away at noon, and we knew that there had been bad trouble for some one, that some one had felt 'the heavy hand, ' and congratulated ourselves that we were but simple troopers, having only to obey, and not to take responsibility of failure. There was a set expression of unfeigning anger that boded ill for some one. The iron jaws were close set, and the seamed face hard with an expression that few men would willingly encounter in their superior.

A sentry by the cottage at Sunnyside, of whom one day we asked directions as to the office of the Military Secretary, had spoken of another phase. Lord Roberts stood in the verandah above the garden, talking to some one earnestly and at length. We had asked the sentry jestingly did he know the Little Man?

"Know 'im! " he replied; "w'y, yuss, I jes' do know 'im. Friend o' the fam'ly, 'e is. Day afore yestiddy, 'e comes along the street on foot, an' w'en 'e gits ter the gite, er course I stan's ter ther 'present'. 'E comes bowlin' in, 's chippy 's if 'e'd bin to a bloomin' dawg-fight. 'Good arternoon, sentry, ' 'e sez, 'any one bin arskin' arter the ole man? ' Blime! I was that took back I 'ardly knows wot ter s'y to 'im. Anyw'y, I manages ter git out as I didn't think no one 'ad called. 'Wot's yer nime, sentry? ' 'e sez. So I tells 'im—nime, an' number, an' regimint. 'Wasn't yer farther with me ter Khanderar? ' 'e sez. Well, Lor lumme! yer could er knocked me hover with a bleedin' swipe—me ole man 'ad bin there, but I didn't think Bobs 'd er mide 'is acquinetance. Well, 'e did. Remembered 'im fer bein' 'colour' in a comp'ny wot 'd done somethink or other. Ain't 'e a nobby little bloke? 'E knows crowds an' crowds er blokes, too—an' yit 'e remembers me ole man, jes' w'en 'e 'ears 'is nime! "

This is quite a true story—at least, if it is not, it is the sentry's lie, not mine. But that is one of the many ways by which Bobs has won the love and esteem of all the army. He never forgets a face or a name, they say, of any one he has had to do with, however humble.

And it is the most wonderful thing in all the world—the way they do love him. To the regular army he is almost a god. One sees his influence everywhere, and one never sees it without some good effect. Of course, we Cornstalks and other outlanders of the Empire only knew him as we saw him in South Africa. A few had read his book, a few had worshipped him afar off always.

But it is Tommy Atkins who knows his true worth best. It is Tommy who speaks most gratefully of the life-work of the Little Man.

For not alone has he been a fighter, though he has seen more fighting than any man alive. There are two rows of ribbons across his jacket. It is not far short of fifty years since he went into action first—since he first heard those whistling noises in the air whose grim import we have learned to recognise but as yesterday, and he has been hearing them ever since.

It is his peace-work, however, as much as his war-work, that has won him the love of all the army. All who read must know of what he has done. We, who have got to know Tommy in some minor aspects of his varied being, can only testify to his grateful appreciation of the efforts of 'Bobs' on his behalf. The common soldier at home must have a bad time of it enough even to-day; but the 'haversack-bred' men whose fathers were in the ranks before them will tell you how much the conditions of barrack-life have improved, even in their remembrance. Especially will you hear this from men who have served in India. And, even in Africa, the Soldiers' Homes he opened—most excellent of institutions upon active service—in each conquered town were of incalculable benefit to all of us. His first and last efforts always seem to be directed towards the amelioration of the conditions under which his soldiers live. And that is one reason why we all loved him so much.

In the fulness of time he will die. He is an old man now, and in a few years—ten or twenty at the very utmost—the hardships of a hardly spent life will have told upon him, iron of brain and constitution though he be. His wars have been wars that have not, at first sight, involved the deaths of mighty empires. There has been no Waterloo for him to win, there has been no lusting ambition in his nature to prompt him to make an Armageddon of his name.

But there is this that may be written in his record—he was a faithful servant of his country, he was a kind master, a humane conqueror, and he was the saviour of the British Empire. Had we lost South Africa we had lost much beside, and it was 'Bobs' alone who saved Africa to us. In his time he has held powers that no king or president of to-day may possess and live. He has held lives in the hollow of his hand; he might have poured out blood in fertile lands as a child pours water from a vessel. But always he has been merciful, always just, always loved by any who have had to do with him—even by his country's enemies—and therein lies his greatness.

CHAPTER XIII - THE ARMY

In the week after the battle of Diamond Hill there were few places in the world where so many varieties of English, so many outlandish men of the Empire, met together and jostled one another as in the streets of Pretoria.

After the short armistice immediately subsequent to the evacuation of the capital by the Boer army and its occupation by that of Lord Roberts, the troops had gone out to surround Louis Botha. It had seemed, at one time in the two days' fighting, that Louis Botha had almost surrounded the troops, but finally, at the expense of many good lives, he had been compelled to retire a little further toward the bush-veldt, northwards. And then the great bulk of the army in the Transvaal sat down in its positions to await the remounts hurrying from the south as fast as the single line of narrow-gauge railway, the exploding culverts, and the ubiquitous De Wet would permit. North, south, east and west, Divisions and Brigades bivouacked in the surrounding veldt. The kopjes about the town were hurriedly fortified and guarded by the invaders against sudden attack. The surrendering of arms, and the merry granting of permits to return to farms, went on as briskly as it had done in the first days after the surrender of Bloemfontein.

Nothing of very much importance was doing anywhere. Baden-Powell from Mafeking, and Methuen from Fourteen Streams, were riding through the Western Transvaal. Paul Kruger administered his vague Government from the migratory saloon carriage on the Laurenco Marques line, and hurled Scriptural exhortation at his dubious burghers. It was a time of stagnation in the north. Below the Vaal the Free Staters were alarmingly active, but here, in our part of the 'Theatre of War, ' nothing more serious went on than the occasional sniping of pickets, and the intermittent cutting-off of small British patrols by the hovering Boer commandos.

And so driblets and details of men 'on leave' from the great chain of outposts about the town were continually coming in to see Pretoria and buy provisions, and the peaceful Dutch capital seemed to have taken on the cosmopolitan air that of right belonged to Johannesburg, thirty miles down the line.

It was a kind of reunion of the army. The many elements that had been drafted off into Brigades and Divisions and composite regiments of sorts—each constituted after its kind—had, as it were, sent delegates to meet informally in Church Street. Groups of men representative of the four quarters of the globe strolled about the quiet streets, filling their haversacks with costly purchases of groceries; raiding the 'Post Kantoor' for stamps of the (almost 'late') South African Republic; visiting the State Museum; peeping into the empty church in the centre of the Market Square; seeking Paul Kruger's house to gape at the Vrouw Kruger; aimlessly wandering all about the town, from the barracks of the Staats Artillerie to the late prison of the English officers in the bird-cage—just as though the place were a resort of excursion trains, and they curious tourists, come for a day to stare about the 'sights'.

Upon the pavements, and in the shops, or gazing curiously into the booksellers' windows where the priceless last issues of the Volkstem and the Standard and Diggers' News were for a little while displayed, were all manner of strange beings, most utterly dissimilar in every aspect, save the outward one of dingy, tattered, march- and battle-stained khaki. There were English Tommies from the counties—sturdy fellows, slow of speech and ponderous of thought; Cockney Tommies from the East of London—slack of manners and gamin-like in bearing; Scotch Tommies who were broad and sturdy, and altogether veritable towers of massive strength; Irish Tommies, whose brogue preceded them round corners; straw-hatted 'handy-men' of the 'Four-point-Sevens, ' who seemed to look with contempt upon the benighted 'soldiers' with whom Fate, for a time, had cast in their lot. There were dainty men of the City Imperial Volunteers; wealthy men of the Yeomanry; men who knew Collins Street; men who had a nodding acquaintance with Sydney, but a close friendship with the Western Plains; Tasmanians, New Zealanders, Queenslanders, Manitobans, men of the North-West, some of Ceylon, Indians, Burmans—all the queer mixture that the Empire had been pouring ceaselessly into South Africa since the war began.

There were little impromptu tea-rooms and hastily improvised coffee-shops, where you might sit at table with them all, where the rich brogue of Limerick mingled with the drawl of Canada and the twang of the Australians—expensive places in which late members of the Boer Army Service Corps and Commissariat departments rapidly grew rich by selling boiled eggs for sixpence, and beef-steaks for half-crowns. In them you might hear the jargons of the trades of nearly all the known universe. Station overseers exchanged views as to grazing with farmers from the Eastern Province. Miners of Kalgoorlie discussed the cyanide process with engineers of the Rand. Policemen of the Klondyke lied against those of Little Bourke Street. Scotsmen fra' Edinboro' 'cracked' wi' those of Otago. Troopers of Cape regiments argued in open Dutch with the proprietors. It was as it had been at Bloemfontein in March, and at Kroonstad in May.

Never again, until the Great War comes, will so many different types of the Empire's soldiery gather together and behold one another. Never again, until then, will there be such an opportunity of comparing the men of the Old with the men of the New World.

Pretoria, in those days, was as a kaleidoscope. All the shifting colours of the race to which we belong blended, and parted, and massed in strange groups, as the bits of glass blend, and mass, and fall apart within the toy. It was a chance to see the world as one had never before seen it, and as one will have a great deal of good luck if one ever sees it again. And, always forcing itself upon one's mind, as one strolled about the streets, was the consciousness of Empire, the vague realisation that we, the English, and the Canadians, and the Australians, were a race that overran the globe, and that its inheritance was ours. Bumptiousness, if you will—but in the midst of that coming together of the Four Corners it was a smugly satisfactory thought that one could not well keep from one's mind. And there was another one, too—less agreeable, but scarcely less forcible—Heavens! Does it take all of us to crumple up two little Dutch Republics lost in the middle of a great continent? This last idea seemed to come as a kind of unpleasant but healthy mental tonic.

To many of us who had never seen him in the mass before, the Englishman was something new. Our ship had come to the South Arm at Capetown Docks, and lain beside a boat-load of Yeomanry. As we drew into the wharf, and lined the taffrail to get a closer view of the land which was to give some of us our graves, there came strolling about the pier strange people in khaki hats and clothing. They were sturdier, fresher complexioned, plumper men than ours— neater in their dress, and less self-assured in bearing. Glancing along the ship's side, one saw a few hundred 'hard' faces peering curiously at all they looked upon, chaffing a sturdy Zulu who deftly manipulated a steel hawser, calling to one another to notice new and striking things, and generally indicating by their manner and bearing that they had assumed ownership over all South Africa, from the Cape Peninsula to the Zambesi, and were just about to take formal possession by stepping ashore. The hardness of the average Australian face had never before come to one so vividly as it did that morning in the docks, when one saw, for the first time, so many ruddy, smooth-faced, flaxen Englishmen beside our lantern-jawed, long-limbed, bark-featured Cornstalks, Crow-eaters and Sand-gropers.

And this is a point amazingly noticeable all through the army of South Africa—that though dress be the same to every button and grease-spot, though arms and equipment may in no wise differ, you will never have the least difficulty in distinguishing a Colonial from an Englishman of England. By 'Colonial' one refers not necessarily to the 'native born, ' but as much to the men who have lived with them for years, and learned their ways and habits in their new land. We had many amongst us who probably had once been as pink and white of countenance as were the Yeomanry.

This is the difference—the Colonial has lived a free life, has had to shift for himself, has been, with more elbow-room, rather more of his own master than has the average Englishman of the same class. In short, the Colonial has had to 'battle' for himself in all respects more than has the Englishman of his kind. And he shows it in his carriage, in his manner, in his very aggressive bearing, and his hardly veiled excellent opinion of himself. He is one of the 'old hands'. The latter is a Jackaroo.

Not that he remains a Jackaroo always. There is no one in the world better gifted by nature to become an 'overseer, ' but here, at the starting-point, in the first experience of open air, he is almost without exception what is known in Australia as a 'New Chum'. And it is so of all the 'Tommies, ' of all the Yeomanry Corps, of all the Volunteers and Militia of England, when good scouting, intelligent dependence upon self, and resource are imperatively required necessities.

One does not say this in any spirit of ill-feeling. Than the Yeomanry one would not wish to meet better fellows, or more agreeable company, and as fighting men—good old English fighting, not the Africander pattern—they are no whit behind (it is even doubtful whether they are not a little ahead of) their brethren of Greater Britain. But in this, and this again—the exercise of what we term 'bushmanship'—until they have learned by bitterly bought experience, they are for ever wanting. Show them their enemy, and they will fight him and 'lick' him—but don't trust them to go and find him themselves, or he will inevitably discover them first, and possibly 'lick' them by sheer wilyness.

As to 'Tommy' himself—who shall speak? He is a class apart, a different species of mankind to any other upon earth. For the sort of man he is, if you wish to learn, you must read Kipling. He knows him, and he has described him as no one else may hope to do.

We had never encountered him before, but we had read our Kipling and were anxiously upon the look-out for what he had taught us to expect. And we found him exactly as described. There were all the strange expressions and twists of speech of Soldiers Three, and many more beside, which no one might render into print. You may trace his origin in his language, and generally it must be low enough. But what seems to one most singular about him is that, out of such material as the recruiting sergeant starts upon, the system makes him into so good a production as it does. It may be stupidity, it may be carelessness, but he is as cheerfully willing to die as any man who lives. It is not his fault that he has no individuality. It is the fault, and at the same time the perfection, of his education—an education which for two hundred years has sternly schooled him not to think, not to suppose that he is even capable of thinking. He is foul-mouthed, he is dull, he is brave, he is patient—he is exactly as one of his own officers is recently reported to have described him—bovine. That word seems to sum him up better than all the pages one might write.

But there is another thing—he has a good heart, he is kind, he is generous, and his public opinion is usually healthy and correct. The following may illustrate his kindliness of heart. Whether it be typical of the whole one is not quite certain, but is almost inclined to believe so.

A few nights after the surrender of Bloemfontein a group of Australian cavalrymen, who were attached as a squadron to a famous dragoon regiment, stood talking about a little fire in the lines at Wessels' Farm. With them were some few of the regiment of which they had the honour to form a temporary part. Some one inquired of another whether he meant to apply for a 'pass' to go into town. "No, " he replied, "what's the use? I'd like to have a look round, but I've got no money! " Nothing more was said at the time, but later, as the group broke up to seek its blankets, one of the 'Greys'—an utter stranger—touched the penniless one upon the shoulder, and whispered to him: "Hey, chom, a can len' ye ten shillin', gin ye wush tae gang t' the toon! "

Could anything have been much kinder? To his credit, the Australian refused the proffered loan.

Of our own immediate kindred there were divers sorts. The men of New South Wales, Victoria, Queensland, South Australia, and Western Australia were all much of a class. One has written of them all practically under the heading of 'Tommy Cornstalk'. They are all mainly sprung from the parent stock of the Hawkesbury and the Hunter, or a common English ancestry, and have the same traditions and characteristics in the main as one another.

The Tasmanians differed, perhaps, a little from the men of the mainland—as Tasmania herself differs from the larger and more modern island continent. One heard of them always as having done good work. They had a commanding officer who seems to have been perpetually 'looking for fight, ' and who kept on looking for it after having been wounded at least twice, if not more often. Tasmania, smallest of all the Australian States, has the distinction of having carried off, so far, all the V. C.'s granted to Australians.

Some Queensland Bushmen who visited our camp near Pretoria had a quaint story of the Victorians, which one would like to believe, but which is scarcely probable. It was to the effect that this particular lot of Banana-landers had gone round to Beira to join Carrington's Rhodesian Column. When they arrived there a steam-launch had come off to the troop-ship, carrying a fat official clothed in white duck. He stepped on deck with all politeness, and inquired beamingly what particular portion of the Empire these so fine soldiers might grace with their presence when at home.

"We're Queensland Bushmen, " they told him.

"Ah—yes—Queenslan', " he said meditatively. "Vell, good morning. I cannot permit you to make to disembark 'ere. You are as ze Veectorians—of Australia, is it not so? I regret ver mooch, but ze Veectorians, zey lan'—zey do what you call sketch—paint ze town red. Not ze bloodshed, I mean. But zey seize ze hotel, drink up all ze beers, an' ze vines, an' ze viskeys. My police expostulate—but zese wild Booshmen, zey seize zem by force, an' place zem in ze preeson, an' make to release all ze preesonaires. No, it is not possible to have more of ze Booshmen of Australia in Beira. Zey are fine fellow, zese Booshmen—but too wil', too wil'. I regret. I sorrow. I wish you a so pleasant voyage back to Capetown. "

The Queenslanders, indeed, returned to Capetown from Beira, and joined in the chase of De Wet, but the reason given as to the Victorians was probably the subsequent production of some fertile brain.

The New Zealanders differed very materially from the 'Cornstalk' troops, however. New Zealand has her own traditions of a fierce and bloody war, which, even though it be of the last generation, is still fresh enough in the memories of the people of to-day to give added soldierly qualities to her sons. They themselves come of a good stock. The climate of the islands is a healthy one. There is something solid and abiding about her people—some stability and sturdiness that, in the smallest degree, is wanting to our possibly more mercurial temperament and constitution.

We of the Australians may all claim proudly that, even apart from our troops having possibly distinguished themselves upon occasion, there has never yet been anything of the wholesale-surrender kind to bring down our average. But the writer does not think than any Australian who has served in Africa will quarrel with him for stating what he honestly believes himself to be true—namely, that of all the troops engaged in this arduous war, none were quite so good as the 'Maorilanders'. Never once, in all the annals of it, did they fail to do the right thing at the right time. Always they were ready when wanted, always to be relied upon in 'tight corners, ' always sure and constant in everything they did.

Not that the others ever wanted either. That was an opinion of Generals and lesser lights in the English army. There was a cossack-post of the writer's own corps, doing duty one day in early April east of Bloemfontein, which was suddenly attacked by a number of Johannesburg Police, who sought to isolate the four men from their main post. They briskly responded to the Boer fire, but, whilst so engaged, their 'linked' horses broke loose, and wandered, all unwitting of danger, to feed upon the scanty grass in front of the little kopje upon which the post was stationed. One of the men thereupon walked down the hill and led the horses round to the back, neither they nor him receiving a scratch though under a fairly hot, if long range, fire. Presently reinforcements came and drove the Zarps away. The English officer in charge of the main post had seen through glasses the risk the men of the cossack-post ran of losing their horses and being themselves cut off, and had come, hot-foot, to their assistance. He was much surprised to find that the horses had been saved. "Ah! " he remarked to the corporal, "you Australians always do well! "

And, though one says it as shouldn't, that was fairly true—but the New Zealanders did, in the humble opinion of the writer at any rate, just a little better.

Of the South African irregular regiments there was one corps to which all others must yield pride of place—that splendid and gallant body of Rand volunteers, the Imperial Light Horse. No corps in all the war has seen quite so much, or done such distinguished service, as this one. They began at Elandslaagte. Some went through the Siege of Ladysmith, and some who had been shut out helped to relieve the beleaguered town with Buller. Then they came round from Durban, and went up to assist Mahon in his notable march to release Mafeking. They came across the Western Transvaal and lost heavily in the fighting about Pretoria in July. Then they went on again towards Delagoa, and, for all the writer knows, may still be riding on the trail of Botha or De Wet. At the end they will have a record second to that of no regiment which has participated either in the Natal or the Western Campaign—and they should never be disbanded. Give the present members of the regiment their discharges, if they wish, but, for the honour of its deeds, keep the I. L.H. upon the shoulder-straps of a body of men in the garrison of South Africa—which, if it comport itself as excellently as did the originally constituted corps, will rival, for efficiency and usefulness, that fine body, the Cape Mounted Rifles itself.

The 'Horse' regiments seemed to be without limit. There were Roberts' Horse, Kitchener's Horse, Marshall's Horse, Brabant's Horse, Nesbit's Horse, Lumsden's Horse, Strathcona's Horse, Paget's Horse, Australian Horse—and many others too numerous to mention. The generality of them were South African corps, formed at the commencement of the war, and supplied with drafts of men from dep'ts in Capetown and Durban, as it progressed.

For some reason or other the Africander regiments were not popular with the troops from over sea—neither Tommies, Australians, nor Canadians seeming to care overmuch about their. That they did splendid service no one can deny. Rimington's Guides, Roberts' Horse, Kitchener's Horse, were always at the front. But there was something that seemed to tell against them in the estimation of their colonial cousins. It may have been that, instinctively, no one quite trusted the Cape Colony. We had come through their people after landing—for the front—and had seen the railway line guarded and patrolled, even into the suburbs of Capetown itself. We had met black looks and ill-concealed dislike at every station on the way to Modder River where the populace were allowed access to the platforms. And so, possibly, there was some feeling regarding these regiments—recruited in what was really an enemy's country, and many of their members having Dutch names—that had given rise to what was, one believes, an wholly unmerited distrust and dislike. Not in any other corps would you hear manifested a so bitter and general dislike of the Boers of both Republics as in these; and there were no troops whom the Boers themselves loathed so venomously as those of the sadly distracted colony. The siege of Wepener, the disaster at Sanna's Post, and half a dozen other hot and unhappy actions, had proved conclusively their loyalty and devotion, and shown beyond any shadow of doubt how well and bravely they could fight and bear themselves. And yet, the Boers hated them with a hatred of disappointment, and the Tommies distrusted them with a pig-headed and unreasoning distrust. Whatever their merits or demerits may have been, the fact remains, however, that they took their fair share of all the burdens of the campaign.

Of all the interesting groups of men who helped to form this strange medley of an army there were none who, for picturesque interest and fascinating detail of exploit, could approach within helio-range of the Canadians. And in this connection the writer has recently been doubting very much whether, in a book that purports to be written by a Cornstalk about Cornstalks, he has not already at various times devoted too much space to the doings of these remarkable men— whether the beguiling shadow of the maple-leaf has not rested too long and frequently upon pages that ought, more properly, to have been chronicles of gum-tree and she-oak men. But, through all the length and breadth of the land, campfire, and hospital, and railway station echoed their weird deeds—they made a name and recollection for themselves within South Africa which will not be forgotten until the race-feud dies out and men cease to speak of nineteen-hundred. Wherever you went, whomsoever you might hold converse with, you heard mention of them. "Have you heard the latest about those hard-cheeked Canadians? " became almost a stock question when conversation flagged, or a new topic were needed. And there was always something fresh or new to tell and hear of them. One seemed to fall, almost unconsciously, under the curious charm of their quaint collective personality. And every one liked them. Undoubtedly they were the most interesting and picturesque figures of the war. Their dashing actions, cool ferocity, quiet 'slimness, ' and guileless 'verneukery' of the Boers themselves—and their pure hard cheek—rendered them famous and fascinating wherever they went.

One has told so often of their prowess and their quaintly serious modes of expression, that there is little left here to explain—but this story of one of them, who out-Canadianed the Canadians, may be worth recording, even though, possibly, it has been told in print before. It is of a man whose renown travelled through all Africa, who, though he was but a corporal of Mounted Infantry, attained a degree of local fame such as some Brigadier might even have envied. It was related to the writer by a Highland officer in Wynberg Hospital, who, having allowed a bullet to pass clean through his head somewhere in that neighbourhood, had been a patient in the hospital at Vredefort, and had himself heard it from both Boer and English sources.

"Well, it seems that this Corporal Clarkson, of the Canadian Mounted Infantry, you know, was rather a noted character in Hutton's Brigade. They used to give him all the hard jobs to do— ridin' out reconnoitrin' by himself, you know, and so forth—and he generally managed to do whatever he was instructed to, and a good deal beside. Sort of 'handy man' at scoutin', you know.

"Well—when French's crowd were just thinking about crossing the Vaal, they camped a few miles outside a little place called Vredefort—typical 'dorp, ' an' all that—you know the kind of thing. Expected a big fight somewhere about, but it didn't come off. So, just to make sure, French thought he'd send some one out to reconnoitre Vredefort. Accordingly, the M. I. were told to find a patrol to do the job.

"Whoever it was had the sending out of the expedition I don't know, but I really think that the man who picked Clarkson to lead must himself have been a born leader of men, you know—sort of chappy who recognises the qualifications of his men, you know, when he wants anything done.

"So, this fellow Clarkson was paraded with five of his 'darned out-fit, ' as those chappies call themselves, you know—and instructed to go and find out whether Vredefort was occupied or not. So out he went.

"When they got to within about a mile of the town, they came quite suddenly over a ridge on to a Boer outpost, or picket, or something—consistin' of eight or ten lusty Dutchmen. Clarkson arrived so very abruptly in their midst, that they hardly knew what was the right thing to do—to shoot or run. Quite flabbergasted 'em, you know. The gallant corporal took in the situation at a glance—let on he was the General himself, you know, and demanded their arms. I think they must have been a lot of awful Johnnies, you know—kind of town guard of Vredefort or something, because they just did as he told 'em. He took their ponies, remounted his men fresh, sent the Boers away on foot, and, leaving two men to guard the loot, continued his advance on Vredefort.

"Well, when he rode into Vredefort, he found the Dutch people fairly scared, you know. They knew French was pretty close, and had been filling one another up with lies about what would happen if he entered the place. There were white flags up on every chimney-pot and gate-post.

"Clarkson simply rode straight up to the office of the Landrost—sort of civil magistrate Johnnie, you know. By this time he was Commander-in-Chief, vice Lord Roberts, resigned; if you give a Canadian an ell he'll take as far as his rifle can carry.

"Our friend simply demanded the surrender of the town—nothing less! Well, the Boer Johnny was so very overcome, you know, and so very much afraid of losing his billet, that he thought perhaps he'd better do as requested, seeing also that Clarkson must undoubtedly be a General of very great standing. So, actin' under orders from Field-Marshal Lord Clarkson, he summoned all the available burghers who had arms to deposit 'em immediately in the Market Square, an' come an' listen to what the great officer of General French had to say. Course, you know, they think French has seniority of God Almighty. Altogether Clarkson collected between forty and fifty Mausers and Martinis, stacked 'em in a waggon, an' sent 'em into Hutton's camp with a note and one of his remaining three men—having previously invited himself to lunch with the Landrost at the hotel. I heard about the note; it was something like this, you know: —

"'Dear General, —Please receive accompanying armament of one commando. I am pleased to state that I have this day captured the city of Vredefort (fancy Vredefort a "city") and taken a large number of prisoners, whom I propose, subject to your approval, to release upon parole. You will be glad to hear that I am at the present moment enjoying an excellent luncheon with the Mayor of this city. We're havin' champagne! After lunch, as to-morrow will be the birthday of Her Most Gracious Majesty Queen Victoria, I propose to formally annex the city to the British Dominions. Hopin' this will find you well, and in good spirits, as it leaves me at present, —I am, dear sir, yours faithfully Duncan Clarkson, Corporal, Canadian M. I.'

"Well, after lunch, he had 'em all called up into the Market Square again. Some English lady had had a flag hidden away all the time, and she produced it for the occasion. So Clarkson commanded the Free State Flag to be hauled down, and ran the Union Jack up in its place.

"Then he made 'em a great speech. Pointed out all the benefits that would accrue to Vredefort under British rule, you know, an' all that—and finally worked 'em up into quite a pitch of enthusiasm, you know, so that they gave three cheers and sang 'God save the Queen, ' etcetera.

"But the best of it, you know, was a snap-shot which that English lady took with a kodak, an' which I saw afterwards. There were all the old Boer Johnnies, you know, cheerin' away like anything, an' throwin' up their hats into the air—our brave boy, seated on his pony in the middle of the crowd of 'em; smilin' like a Cheshire cat, and—with one hand on the butt of his revolver!

"Well, now, I call that 'moral suasion, ' don't you? "

And now we will leave the Canadian, and the Africander, and the Yeomanry, and the Tommies, and all the great gathering of the Empire's outmost outposts in all their diversified glory, and consider briefly another matter that is of some moment to us who helped to earn it—the reputation of the army.

In Pretoria, one morning, the writer had an opportunity of conversing with an Irish-American who had served under the redoubtable Blake, 'Colonel' of the Boer-Irish Brigade, and, being disgusted with that worthy person, and 'full-up of fighting, annyway, ' had surrendered his Mauser and was for compulsory deportation shortly. Had been, he said, a burgher of the Transvaal. Had been, also, at Ladysmith, Colenso, and on the Tugela, and was, on the whole, rather a decent fellow—very different to the stray prisoners of Blake's disreputable command whom one had hitherto encountered. It was not "Go to hell! " with him to every question asked.

He had fought with the Boers because he had believed, and still believed, in the justice of their cause. And then he told the horrible story which one fancies that delightful gentleman, Mr. Michael Davitt, was the first to 'father' in print. It was the old Boer anecdote about the patrol of brutal lancers in Natal, who, being in the debatable lands foraging, had incontinently misused a farmhouseful of Dutch women and girls to such a dreadful extent that some of them had lost their reason, and one had died. And he believed it.

Well, there have been stories printed in our own papers as to frightful Boer atrocities—wretched crimes such as you would not book to black fellows—which have received only too ready credence in the public mind of England and the Empire. And if you get files of last year's Standard and Diggers' News, you will find that just the same kind of stories were served out, hot and smoking, to the people of the late Republics. You may believe them or not, as you please. No one can actually dispute them now, even if one wished to take the trouble. It is one of the most miserable features of war—the malevolent lying that takes place upon both sides—not so much among the actual combatants as between the skulkers behind each respective army. Personally, one believes no worse thing of the Boers than of our own people. There are blackguards in every army, but in most you will find, if you look below the surface, that public opinion is astonishingly healthy.

But this much one may say, and say with no fear of contradiction by those who are competent to judge—that the British Army, as a whole, was precisely what Lord Roberts described it as being—"an army of gentlemen".

If you do not judge a man by the fit of his clothes, or whether he eat appallingly with his knife, or make weird noises as he absorbs soup, you will look to the broad principles of his larger actions when you wish to classify him as either 'gentleman' or 'blackguard'. And, regarding the whole mass of the soldiery of the Empire, both regular and volunteer, who fought in South Africa—one may say unhesitatingly that they certainly did not behave as 'blackguards'. We may have used bad language, we may have done a little looting, or used 'moral suasion' when we starved, but never once did the writer, in all the marching between Paardeberg and Nitral's Nek, see, or hear of, one case of a woman, black or white, being maltreated or mishandled in any way. And it was not for lack of opportunity. It was not, perhaps, because there were not men amongst us who would stick at nothing in the satisfaction of their more brutal inclinations. But it was because of this—that an Englishman is an Englishman, a Canadian a Canadian, an Australian an Australian, a White Man a White Man all the world over, and that, wherever the leader of any army sets his face sternly against brutality or inhumanity, then there will be little or none of either.

And so, again, writing as one of the humblest 'rankers' in it, one may agree with the Great Little Man who led it, that the South African Field Force was an army of gentlemen.

CHAPTER XIV - THE BOER

"Fetch us Kruger's scalp! " said the crowd that lined the streets, as we struggled hotly to Woolloomooloo Bay on a sweating afternoon in January. "Don't take any notice of white flags; play 'em at their own game; wipe 'em out; give 'em hell! " —they cried as we led our horses up the gangway. "Good-bye, boys, " screeched an excited lady on the wharf; "put their blanky lights out! "

There had been Stormberg, and Magersfontein, and Colenso—and Spion Kop was to come. The facile pen of the paragraphist had described the incidents of treacherous ambush. The tame leader-writers of the most respectable morning paper in the wide world had, with all deference to possible varieties of opinion—which they would not for all the riches of Mount Morgan unwittingly offend— given it as their unalterable dictum that the Boer was an excrescence upon the fact of all humanity, that he should, without doubt, be made to feel the 'iron hand, ' that this war was none of your common, bloody, uninviting struggles, but a holy crusade against infamous wrong, and injustice, and unreasonable tyranny. Most touchingly symbolical of its righteous approval of our going, the enthusiastic crowd had given us to drink of raw whisky, as we shoved, and pushed, and panted thirstily through it. And doubtful damsels, to whom one would never before have attributed any of the broad feeling that leads to publicly expressed emotion, had clung weepingly about our necks, and kissed us lovingly, as they implored us to go forth and battle for what was right, and good, and noble, against oppressive wrong and wretched, heartless cruelty.

And so, by the time that we were up the shrouds, and the crowd was a mere blur along the shore, expressive only by points of waving white and a murmuring roar that lost itself across the widening waters, we really did feel enthusiastic admiration for ourselves. We honestly understood ourselves to be, as it were, knights-errant of no mean order, going forth to wrest the fair maiden of African freedom from the vile clutches of the Boer dragon.

It was a splendid feeling to possess—you can have no idea as to how very noble and estimable our souls felt themselves to be. The Holy Grail itself was in Pretoria, or Johannesburg, and we were going to get it.

Tommy Cornstalk

In Adelaide the people had again gone mad. Men of the Stock Exchange—fat, worthy members of Society—had clutched us frantically by the arms, and given us to drink of choice vintages. The North Terrace and the railway station had farewelled us with more delightful fervour than even if we had been an Australian Eleven driving round in drags, ere it sought Largs Bay and the track to victories in English cricket-grounds. Fremantle had been a little madder. Truly, it was something to be a soldier.

And we sailed away knowing all about everything. There was no possibility of our having made any mistake as to the Boer. We had him at our finger ends. He was a low liar, a cunning, unscrupulous cheat, an oppressor of the unfortunate philanthropists who had come to make his country rich.

The Uitlander, for whom we were going to do battle, was indeed a long-suffering, overburdened martyr. Purely for philanthropy he had sought to do the Transvaal a good turn. He had toiled, with some success, to wrest the golden treasure of the unwilling Rand from its hidden depths. He had made a bankrupt State into a rich one. He was the kind of man who shoved the world along. And they wouldn't give him a vote. So we were going to get it for him. The Boer had been weighed in the balance and found wanting. We would adjust the scale.

And even as we thought we were right, and just, and ethically correct in assisting the mother country to make war in Africa, so do we still to-day—after we have been, and learned what war really is, and sobered ourselves in scenes of misery from the drunkenness of the 'hurrahing' streets, and the hysteric quays, and the lying newspapers. But it is upon other grounds that we so justify ourselves. And we have learned to think a little differently of the Boer.

There is a dreadful crime against all moral decency, a hopeless offence against all that is right, and just, and proper. It is so serious an offence that one may reasonably hesitate before laying oneself open to the charge of having been guilty of it. In its most abandoned state of depravity and perversion it does not merely suggest, it confirms and makes positive the fact that the offender against all good and worthy codes of political thought is a treasonable plotter and outcast conspirator against his country too. He is an enemy of England, an insidious foe to the welfare of the Empire. He has

141

committed the unpardonable sin. Henceforth he should be treated mercilessly as a pariah. He is an 'Ishmael' amongst his fellows. He is incapable of reason—he is hopelessly insane. We should 'cut' him in the street, if he be an acquaintance. We should bestir ourselves to put him down, to expose him, to hold him up to ridicule, to make his life a weary burden. He is not even worth reforming.

And so the writer hopes, and prays, and ponders within himself as he writes—almost overwhelmed by the nightmare fear that he may be charged, too, with this unspeakable wrong-doing, that little boys, and old women, and worthy men may arise and point the finger of scorn at him, and damn him, soul and body, with the awful accusation of 'Pro-Boer'.

It is so easy to have this cry hurled at you. You have but to say that the African Dutch do not all live in pig-styes, that some few of them can read and write, that there are even some who do not play with white flags perpetually. To assert that the Devil is not so black as he is painted is wicked and untrue—because every one knows that he is as black as black can be, even though no one has seen him.

Well—but it can't be helped. With a full knowledge of all the dreadful meaning of 'Pro-Boer, ' and what he lays himself open to by reason of his saying so, the writer cannot but state that, as we found him, the Boer was not such a bad fellow after all—not nearly so black as he has been painted. He was, indeed, not one whit better than he should have been, but, in the actual waging of war, he was not nearly so bad as he might have been.

Books, and magazines, and newspapers had almost taught us to believe that we should meet in Africa some kind of a sub-tropical Esquimo—a hairy, primitive 'loafer, ' with the manners of a cave-dweller and the principles of a gorilla. We had looked for a species of debased creature unpossessed of any powers of thinking, with no perception of anything that lay beyond the narrow horizon of his straitened intellectual outlook. We had taken 'Boer' to be synonymous with 'boor'. We had been unable to understand why, or how, he had made matters so uncomfortable at Magersfontein for such men as the Highlanders, led by such skilled and quick-witted men as we had supposed the English officers to be. It was inexplicable to us how such a creature could possibly have 'enough in him' to make the Empire look so foolish as he had undoubtedly been doing for the few months in which it had waged war with him.

Buller was to have eaten his Christmas dinner in Pretoria. It seemed to be rather by good luck than anything else that Joubert was prevented from eating his in Durban.

Now, how could it come about that such a people as these were said to be—a so slow, dull, unprogressive, shiftless people—could give our armies so much trouble, could kill our men by the hundred, and capture them by the thousand? When we made the better acquaintance of the Boer we learned why it was.

It is a far cry from Fremantle to the Orange River. You have time to think and consider matters, with a good deal of attention to detail, in the time that elapses between your departure from one and your arrival at the other. There is the blue solitude of the Indian Ocean, for two clear weeks at least, and after that the speedless journey in the train. But it was first at Orange River station that we made the acquaintance of the Boer in any quantity, and it was there that we first began to doubt the fixity and unchanging nature of our ideas about him. There, too, we first had a glimpse of insight as to the reasons why he had given our Generals and their armies such a deal of trouble.

When our long string of cattle-trucks containing horses, and second-class carriages containing Cornstalks, had jolted and bumped into the station, they had relegated us to a siding, and left the main line beside the platform clear and open—evidently for a more important train than ours. In course of time it had rolled in beside us, and from our windows we looked out upon an excursion train-load of shearers, or 'cockies, ' or ordinary 'bush hands' going down, en masse, with their coats off, to 'blue their cheques'. But in each carriage was the glimmer of bayonets, and, as the train stopped, more bayonets came along beside the carriages and took up positions of vantage in the space between us.

Who were these people? Ah! possibly the poor of Kimberley just relieved, and being taken to Capetown for a change. No, that couldn't be correct. Were they Boers? we ventured to ask the supporter of a bayonet below our window.

"Yes, they be Cronjy's men—seven hundred of 'em, an' they stinks 'orrid. "

Boers! —Boers! —these men Boers? Oh, no; they could not be, surely! Where were the brutal faces of the English illustrated papers? There were a few, a very few, who came up to our conception of a Boer, but the majority seemed decent, intelligent men enough. Their clothes were dirty and clay-stained. They wore moleskins, and riding breeches, and weather-worn tweed coats, and their beards were mostly untrimmed, but where were the 'wild-men-from-Borneo' kind whom we knew well were the only genuine Boers? A great proportion of their train-load were beardless boys or venerable greyheads. Where were the savage beast-like creatures whom we knew we should expect? These men could not be the real Boers. They were not at all like the pictures we had seen.

But, yes—there was no doubt. These were the men from Paardeberg. These were the ferocious creatures who had lived for more than a week upon the smell of lyddite fumes, in a place that was the first cousin to the Hobs of Hell. These boys, and patriarchs, and smaller proportion of able-bodied men, had indeed seen more than ever we had done of war, and felt its cruel weight more heavily than we hoped would fall to our lot to feel. These quiet, orderly, rather good-humoured people! We watched their train roll away with a curious feeling of having been somehow deceived.

Yes, those were the Boers of Boerdom—Transvaalers mostly, who were reputed to be even more wild and unkempt than the Freestaters, who lived very close to the Basutos, and might reasonably be supposed to have acquired their ways. Somehow we were disappointed in them. It was rather like going to see some much advertised entertainment, and finding, when you had paid your money and gone inside, that the reality fell very far short of the posters. We had seen infinitely better specimens of the real Boer in some of the back creeks and dark gullies at home on the Hunter.

And so we went on, and finally, at the end of months, we came to Pretoria—much more educated people than when we had shipped ourselves at Woolloomooloo. We had fought him, chased him, taken him prisoner, narrowly escaped from the tricky snares he set for us, seen him in his home, drawn his fire from his own beloved kopjes, played him at his own game, looked upon his dead—and our opinion of him was quite a different matter altogether from the ideas with which we had equipped ourselves before leaving Sydney. We had seen how he lived; we had learned what manner of slothfulness had kept him from using aright the good land which God had given him, and recognised how little he deserved to keep it therefore—since no man has a right to any good thing unless he use it well. We had talked and argued with him, had got to know his peculiar ways of thinking, had faintly understood his mental state, had discovered for ourselves some of his many faults, had seen how the white flag trick was played—and—one confesses it almost apologetically in view of the possible charge of 'Pro-Boerism' referred to above—had come to respect him, in the mass, as a very gallant man, and to envy in him the possession of hardy virtues such as we had never expected to find, and which we would not mind feeling quite sure that we possessed ourselves.

There lives upon the outskirts of Pretoria, in a little iron cottage, a gaunt old Boer of many years and much experience, with whom the writer chanced to become, in a measure, friendly—as friendly as any hated rooinek may become with one of his uncompromising sort. He was a tall, dark man, grizzled and iron-grey, with the whipcord neck muscles that you see in thin old men who have lived much in the sunlight. He was as spare, and lank, and brown as any Queenslander. And he loved his country with a fervent love that would hear no evil of it. He seemed to like speaking about its troubles to any one who would listen, and was pitiably anxious to make at least one 'Englander, ' as he included all of us, think less hardly of his people than he supposed they did.

Sitting in the shade of a paling fence, we discussed many things through rank clouds of Transvaal tobacco. He had been a fighting man all his life, but had come home when Pretoria fell—stiff with rheumatism—to find his wife but just recovering from the shock of his reputed death whilst on commando, and his little daughter seven weeks dead of typhoid. So there was to be no more war for him, though he never would admit the overthrow of his beloved Republic. Were not the Russians at war with England over China? Would they not bombard Capetown and Durban? Were not the Cape Dutch about to rise, and cut us off from the sea?

He had been at Bronkhurst Spruit in '81, and over the crest of Majuba in time to see Colley fall. His story of the storming of Majuba was curiously interesting.

"Ja! in the morning, there were the English above us. We could see them walk about and stand against the sky. The Boers they were all frighten'. It was bad, very bad. Piet Joubert was angry. He call us young men to him, and he say: 'This is not good. You have not done well. I am angry for it. You have let rooibaatjes come up there, and now you must drive them down again. ' Ja—he was very angry—the so careful Piet. So we went up. No, there were not so many tree—a few bushes, and many rocks, and the grass was long. We take a long time, and it was very steep. But we go so carefully, so very slowly, from rock to rock. They stand up to shoot us, and we shoot them— so. Ah, you do not have the white hats now, or red coats! It is not so easy. We get up close, very close—the officers come and stand against the sky to shoot their pistols at us. We laugh, and shoot them. It is so funny, what you English did in that war. You play bands when you fight. That is wrong. It is not hard to hear the bands coming. And the flags to shoot at! It is not so now. But we come to the top of the kop, and they are all together like frightened buck— — " But it was not a pleasant story. And Bronkhurst Spruit was less so.

There was much to learn from the old man. He would admit many things. Personally, he deplored the white flag incidents, but stoutly maintained that our guns had shelled their ambulance waggons. He was willing to admit that distance does not sometimes help to distinguish an impromptu hospital van from an ammunition cart, but claimed the same reason for occasional lapses on the part of the Staats Artillerie. For the white flag he shrugged his shoulders. "If I steal oxen, it is not that every one in the country will steal oxen too. There are bad men always. I know the commandants do not like it. Louis Botha it has sometimes make very angry. But the Boers have not orders like the English. Every burgher does as he wishes. It is not always possible to watch them all. I have not done it. "

As to expanding ammunition, he made a statement which startled the writer.

"Ah, yes, " he said, "you say we have used it! So—we have done so—but why? I will tell you why—and then you shall tell me what you think. When we drive the English from Dundee, to shut them up in Ladysmith, they go so very quick that they have not time to take all with them. They do not even have time to burn all that they leave behind. So, we find biscuits, and beef, and whisky—ja! —plenty of things that are very good for us. And also there is much ammunition in boxes—what you call it, sof' nose, eh? Dum-dum? Almighty! I tell you, the Boers are very angry. They say, 'If the English use it, we shall use it too! Why not? It is right for us, if it is right for you. ' I think myself it is bad to use—but if you, then the Boers also. We know you use it first of all, because we find it in Dundee when the English have trekked away so quickly. What of that, tell me, mine friend? "

His friend could not explain. Was it that, in the hasty retreat of Yule's column, the possible Dum-dum ammunition brought from India by the troops which came from there at the earliest outbreak of hostilities, and withdrawn from them, as we know it was, had been by some oversight left undestroyed in store at Dundee? That seemed to be the only explanation, but, unfortunately, it did not find ready acceptance with the Boers. The writer rashly questioned a Commandant in Wynberg Hospital as to the same thing, and, to his humiliation, heard the same depressing story.

Expanding ammunition, one is quite certain, was never countenanced by the British authorities; but it is always possible to suppose that our own men, finding it in the bandoliers of dead Boers, may have used an occasional cartridge without their officers' knowledge.

Of Boer inhumanity we have heard many stories. Some of them may possibly be true. Any story is true until it is disproved, despite the English maxim as to a man's innocence being taken for granted until his guilt be clearly established. That may hold good in law, but it does not in scandal-mongering. But this much the writer can unhesitatingly affirm—that, though he read many accounts in English and Australian newspapers of dastardly acts committed by the Boers upon prisoners and wounded, he never once, whilst at the front, could learn of any genuine instance where such things happened. Indeed, men of his own corps, who were wounded and taken prisoners at Zand River in May, speak gratefully of the kind treatment meted out to them by their captors. One is inclined to believe that much of the odium cast upon the Boers arises from the unfortunate lying that seems to be engendered in a war, upon both sides.

But, even admitting that there may be a foundation of truthfulness in much that has been charged against them, there is one unhappy fact which it would be well for us to recollect, and that is that to the average Boer an Englishman is a being who ranks lower than a Kaffir. He is one to whom, if you may do so safely, you may quite permissibly extend the harshest treatment. No one who has not spoken with them, and had opportunity of gathering some notion as to the hatred and contempt and distrust with which they regard everything English, can quite realise this in its full significance.

One day a patrol of Australians, riding through the country between Boesman's Kop and the Bloemfontein waterworks, called at a farmhouse to see whether its members could purchase anything in the way of provisions. There were no menkind there except a couple of Kaffir 'boys'. The mistress of the house could only sell them a glass of milk each, which they were glad enough to get. Afterwards, in course of conversation, she admitted that she was sick of the war, and expressed a fervent wish that it would soon be over. Her husband was away on commando, and her eldest son—a boy of fifteen—had been killed at Modder River. Of her husband she had had no word for three months. He had gone northward in the flight from Bloemfontein, and, for all she knew, might be dead also. Some one asked her how she thought the English and Dutch would get on with one another—would they forget all past ill-feeling, and settle down quietly and happily together for the good of the country when once the war was over? Had she herself anything against the English? "Ah, no, " she said bitterly; "I have not anything against them—oh, no—they have only killed my little Piet! That is nothing. My man's oxen are all gone—that also is nothing! " Then, with sudden fierceness, pointing to the child on her lap, "You see my little girl here; well, if I ever thought she would grow up and marry one of your English, I would take her now and dash her brains out against the door-post! "

That is how they hate us. And it will be many years before the hatred dies away. Blood is a hard thing to forget. The smell of it remains with you afterwards. Wives who have lost their breadwinners, mothers who have lost their sons—be they Dutch or English—do not reason overmuch about the ethics of their losses. It is nothing to them whether the war was a just one, whether their beloved died for a righteous cause. They only know that the cruel English, or the cruel Dutch, have robbed them of some one whom all the fine arguments in the world will not bring back, and so, for years and years, the sad women of those countries will loathe and detest all things English more bitterly than before. Their hatred of us already dates from before the Great Trek, from before the hanging of Slachter's Nek, and comes across the war of '81. Now it will have all the hard misery of this war to add to its rankling bitterness. There is a difficult task before the coming rulers of the two late Republics.

And so, when we hear that the Boers have been unduly lax in honourable dealings with our kinsfolk, we must remember how they regard them. What an invasion and conquering of our country by Chinese would mean to us, the invasion and taking of theirs by the English means to them.

A state of war does not usually exhibit the non-combatants of an invaded country to their best advantage, although naturally there are many opportunities for the display of heroism and self-sacrifice of a high order. The type of Boer with which one came in contact was not always the best. He was usually a prisoner, or sick or wounded in hospital, or one of those not very noble beings — a burgher-on-parole. One cannot but feel the highest personal respect for the men who have uncompromisingly kept the field, as contrasted with those who have surrendered early, and are busily employed in making money out of their country's enemies. But, as a rule, one finds them such an interesting and many-sided people, that there is some regret at not having made their acquaintance years ago in peace-time, so that one might be the better qualified to judge of them. They have, one suspects, been frequently the victims of too hasty judgment. It would possibly have been easier to understand them better, had one been able to mix with them in their laagers. But, in the marching and fighting of the war itself, one was really able to make only a superficial acquaintance with them. Their habits of cunning warfare were really their most striking characteristic. And these taught you, that in Africa one must always be ready to distrust the obvious. Perhaps, indeed, that is one explanation of their noted 'slimness'.

Of Paul Kruger, and the Pretoria clique, and Dr. Leyds the writer knows little save what he has read. Better informed people have dealt with them. But this much is quite certain — that no matter how the Pretorian party plotted, or the Africander Bond dabbled in treason in the Cape Colony, the commoner Boer knew only that he fought for his independence. And Boer independence in South Africa does not merely mean autonomy for the two Republics. It means one Dutch State, and no English, save on sufferance. Knowing this, can we not extend some generosity of feeling towards brave men, who have fought pluckily against overwhelming forces in what was, to them, a sacred cause?

The writer hopes sincerely that this chapter may not draw upon him the reader's scorn and contempt as being another of those strange people — the 'Pro-Boers'. But possibly the fact of having 'chanced one's hide' a few times in action with them will render apology needless. One has small sympathy with Englishmen who, once the country having been involved in war, wilfully admire and encourage the enemy. 'A long rope and a short shrift' for those who are traitors to their country is unfortunately out of date. This much he would be glad if he could feel that he may possibly have made clear in the foregoing pages—that because you are at war with a people it makes your case no better to libel them; that there are as likely to be justice and reason upon their side as yours; that, even if you kill a country, there is no reason why you should traduce its memory also.

One might write indefinitely as to the Boers. From the point of view of the picturesque, at least, they are worth ten volumes, rather than one meagre chapter. But here space forbids.

Let us, however, try to remember so much as this. These people are much of the same kind as we. They have the open air to live in just as we have. They are not monsters of iniquity and treachery altogether. They have fought bravely and well against odds that might have well overwhelmed them in the contemplation—and it was not because they were ignorant. They may be liars by nature, they may be cunning, they have not used their country as they might have done. We were quite justified in fighting them to a finish—but let us at least act the manly part of giving them what credit is their due, of refusing to believe the cruel lies which interested parties have put forth. Let us be fair, and just, and generous—if we can.

CHAPTER XV - THE END

"An unhappy land"—no phrase or words could possibly sum up the situation of South Africa to-day better than these, none could have a deeper or sadder meaning to any one who has seen recently the bitter distraction of all the country there. It is a land drenched with the best blood of its people, and with the best of ours; a land ravaged, and wasted, and made empty; a land afflicted with the curse of the soldier from end to end. It is as a grievously sick man, who is incapable of earning his own living, and has to be supported by some one else. There is nothing there. Its industries are man killing and maiming; its exports are human lives.

Take the train at Kroonstad and journey to the Vaal. It is not very far, but you will not travel so quickly that you may not look out and see for yourself how the land lies. You will pass out of Kroonstad with a great canvas hospital upon your left. Blue-clad, miserable men will listlessly take stock of your train as it passes by. Up above the white tents, on a little slope of open veldt, you will see rows of mounds. Perhaps the grass has grown over some of them by now. They were bare and new when the writer came by six months ago. You will run past America and Jordaan Sidings—empty voids, where nothing but a station signboard notifies the fact that they have been stopping-places for trains in some other age. You will pass over culverts and little bridges that have been blown up with dynamite, and rapidly repaired out of old sleepers and nondescript material of all kinds by that wonderfully efficient Railway Pioneer Regiment. At frequent intervals there will be twisted rails and partially burned sleepers beside the tracks—no, on second thoughts, there will be no sleepers, because the patrols will have garnered them up for fuel. Sometimes you will come across wrecked and burned railway trucks and other rolling-stock.

At little stations, such as Honing Spruit, you will find all manner of curly and angular entrenchments and gun emplacements, and redoubts, and far out sangars for the outposts, and a bewildering entanglement of encircling barbed wire. And there will be harassed officers, and empty tins of bully-beef, and discontented 'Tommies, ' and a demand for news.

At Roodeval you will see the row of seven graves beside the line— each one ornamented with its wooden cross, and caps and sides of nine-inch shells, and little surrounding borders of stones. And, out across the veldt, you will see the places where Christian De Wet planted his guns, and shelled the Fourth Derbyshire beyond all endurance. By this time the half-burned letters from the captured mail-bags will hardly be so much in evidence as they were in August of last year, and the acres of fire-destroyed khaki clothing will not be at all noticeable.

At the Kopjes Siding you may possibly come across an armoured train, with its 'pom-pom' on the leading truck, and its steel-lined trucks for men, and boiler-protected engine, and air of readiness for sudden call. Its crew will be playing football in the veldt. But they won't be very far away from their rifles and bandoliers of cartridges. It is inexpedient to be overdistant from your rifle in this part of the world.

But one common feature of the landscapes which you pass through will probably strike you much more forcibly than any other. You will wonder what may have become of the population, the dwellers in the veldt, the obviously inevitable inhabitants whom such a good country should support. You will perceive that the veldt is dotted at intervals with white houses, which are sometimes shaded by the blue-green gum leaves you know so well. You will be at a loss to understand why no one lives in them, why there are no flocks of sheep about the downs, or herds of cattle drinking at the dams. It will strike you that the only stock in this country are Mounted Infantry ponies.

Sometimes, however, as you pass a house that is closer to the railway-line than usual, you will perceive the reason of this dearth of population. The windows are empty and gaping. The roof is gone. Broken pieces of furniture and household effects litter the ground in front and rear. There is nothing left. To live in such a place would not be at all comfortable. One or two will have shell-holes in the walls. If you get out of your carriage and look very closely you will be able to find little chipped holes in the white-washed mud plaster of the walls, where the bullets have struck.

And that is the way it is everywhere. These places along the line have been burned and destroyed in accordance with the warning Lord Roberts gave the inhabitants as to raids upon his communications. It is quite fair and legitimate, generally speaking. We must establish British rule—gently, if possible, but it must be established. Away from the line, too—if you have not seen enough to prove to you that this is 'an unhappy land'—you will find the burned and empty houses, the impoverished farms. It cannot be helped. We have tried lenient measures—a leniency which only returned to us in derision. These people are obstinate. We mean to have our way. They must be made to feel that the yoke will weigh heavily until our way is theirs also.

But it is cruel—bitterly, heartrendingly cruel!

It is not only in the gutted dwellings that you will see the cruelty and horror of it all. Go back from the Vaal to Bloemfontein, and walk to the cemetery below the old fort and beside the barracks of the late Free State Artillery. You will find some graves of British soldiers which have been occupied since the early fifties, but you will find them vastly outnumbered by the graves of those who found a resting-place there in 1900.

Of coming from a visit to some sick comrades in the Artillery Barracks, which were then occupied by the Australian Hospital, the writer has one very vivid recollection. Walking beside the graveyard wall, we had paused to watch the burial of some officer, which was a little more noticeable than the generality of funerals for the reason that his body was enshrouded in a Union Jack instead of a brown blanket. We mounted our horses, and rode round the corner of the stone enclosure. At the gate were lying on the grass six stiff shapes, sewn tightly up in their blankets—probably the blankets they had died in. The fatigue parties within were so busy that, for a few minutes, they had not had time to come out and carry the dead men in, and the cart, probably being required to go to another hospital for a similar load, had had to deposit them outside. It was a grim reminder of the brisk business Death was doing amongst the enteric wards.

In course of time the pretty burial-ground was filled to overflowing. There were long trenches in which the dead were laid in layers. A separate grave was a luxury to which none but an officer might aspire. And before very long the trenches were being dug in the veldt without the town.

Ride up the Modder and track the march of the army by the graves. Note the little mounds along the advance to Pretoria. Chance on quiet beautiful places like Nitral's Nek, and find them sown with dead men. Everywhere there are dead men. It is as if the whole country were soaked in blood, and planted with little wooden crosses. Truly, it is 'an unhappy land'.

Now, if you consider all these matters of graves, and burned farmhouses, and how very greatly women influence the lives of men in their capacity of motherhood, you will see quite plainly what an exceptionally curious state of mind South Africa must be in at present, and how difficult it is for any one to predict what the finality of it all may ultimately be.

Have you ever seen a somewhat spoiled and wilful child, strongly desirous of doing or obtaining something which is not good for him (there are so many things), finally restrained from the attainment of his end by sheer physical fear? The moment authority relaxes, the instant the back of the power that overawes him is turned, you may feel quite certain that he will attempt the fulfilment of his wish. In the meantime, while he is watched and guarded, and because he dare not do as he would, he has an attitude of sulky acquiescence— he is sullen. There you have a simile that may stand for the mental state of the people of the two late Republics, and for their kinsmen of the Cape Colony as well. And there, too, you have the great difficulty of future government in South Africa.

We have taken the country again. We are about to rule it again, and as we rule it so will it prosper. One does not use the word 'prosper' to signify that there will be a larger output of gold from the Rand, or that the De Beers Company will get bigger dividends out of Kimberley, but that the country may become a country of good citizenship, of healthy public spirit, of fellowship of the two almost kindred races which will have to live together in it. And, to this end, we must be firm yet kind, strong but gentle, just if stern—but, above all, consistent in our dealings with these people from whom we have taken their nationhood in open fight.

We have the mistakes that brought about the Great Trek, and the humiliations of '81 and '99, to guide us towards better things—to show us, at the least, 'the way not to do it'. And if you know that, the rest is not so very difficult of attainment—only, you must first of all know that. Before everything, one thinks, the watchword should be 'consistency'.

And what a hope there is for a new, a 'reconstructed' South Africa! Blood has been spilt as water, treasure scattered lavishly as lucerne seed, brain energy dissipated as a spendthrift's money. Are we not to have a return? To those of us who have seen the misery of the country as it is to-day—the empty void the war has made of it—it seems impossible that there can be any blacker depth to reach. The tide has sunk to its lowest ebb. Of the very nature of things it must soon begin to rise again. In the earlier chapters of this book, the writer has hazarded it as his insignificant opinion that the country is a good one—he is even doubtful whether, if the matter were to be fully considered by people more competent of judging its merits than he is, it might not almost be ranked, for many purposes, as a better one than Australia. It is, as has been said before, even as a field that has been uncultivated. It has its disadvantages and drawbacks, but one is very doubtful, indeed, whether it has so many or such appalling ones as we have encountered and overcome here, or as confront us even now. It has a soil that is, best for best, as good, and it has a rainfall that is better. So, let our châteaux d'Afrique be pleasant ones if we may do so. After having seen the poor rent and riven land wallowing in such depths of misery as it has lain in, it is at least a cheerfully optimistic feeling to possess about it 'that there is a good time coming' for the Cape, the Orange River Colony and the Transvaal. They will surely need it to compensate for the bad one they have had. Let us hope, therefore, that out of much evil there will come good for South Africa, that, in the future, one may think of her less sadly than in the present—that in the end she may be 'a happy land'.

To us of Australia this has been the first experience of war. Far away from the complications of European politics, we have been permitted, for the century or so of our existence, to develop our country upon peaceful lines, and beyond, 'for the look of the thing, ' mounting obsolete artillery at a few points along our shores, where no one is ever likely to attempt to invade us, we have not thought it worth our while to give overmuch attention, in a serious way at any rate, to the possible contingency of having to fight for our country, in just as desperate and bloody a fashion as the Boers have had to fight for theirs.

But we are nearer to the centre of the whirlwind now than we were in '54—just a little nearer than we were in '85. And though, knowing now what W-A-R spells, one has the devout and fervent hope that we may never more fully realise the significance of the word in our own good land, it is absolutely necessary, for the sake of our existence as the Nation which we became a few months ago, that we should be at all times fully competent to maintain our position in the wider arena within which peoples and races shape their destinies in the struggle for existence.

If the reader shall have done the writer the honour of wading through these pages of chaotic scribbling so far as this one, the latter is not going to take any mean advantage of him by seeking to inflict his views as to the superiority of Mounted Infantry to Cavalry, the moral effect of quick-firing guns and the mobility of artillery, or the faults of present systems of military organisation and equipment upon him. Many more competent, and many quite as incompetent people have already laid the law down as to all manner of military matters. It is easy to criticise, as has been before remarked with regard to the Hospitals, but very hard to suggest reasonably.

But, if he may be permitted here, in the last pages of his book, to point out one obvious lesson that may be drawn for Australia from the history of the English struggle with the Boers, he would very much like to set it forth. Without overmuch wearisome preamble it may be suggested by the one word — Ammunition.

If we have cartridges we have men who can use them effectively; but if we have none, then we are 'a gift' to the first hostile Power who may seek to take us.

So, this is the lone suggestion which the writer ventures to make, knowing that he is too ignorant and impracticable to fully elaborate the scheme. That we build ourselves a small-arm ammunition factory somewhere by the Canoblas, and make some cartridges, and keep on making them, until we have so many millions that we may afford to bury them in handy places about the country, after the manner of Christian De Wet and other gifted Generals who know what they are about, and whose heads are 'screwed on the right way'. And then, when the Great War comes suddenly (as it will come when it does come), we shall feel safe, and happy, and content to rely upon ourselves, even though all those slim, untried ships in Farm Cove strew the beaches from Byron Bay to Gabo.

Of course, we need rifles also — plenty of them — and would be all the better off did we make them, too — but we should have, first and above all, enough cartridges to make our supply inexhaustible, and the means of keeping it so when we shall have been cut off from English importations. Cannon, also, and shells, we might make—but that is too vast a dream, perhaps; and, after all, if we have cartridges and rifles, and men who know how to shoot, we may laugh at all the 'shrapnel' and 'common-shell' that were ever made for Krupp or Creusot guns. While we can arm such men as those who defied De la Rey at Eland's River we need have little fear for the safety of our country, but if we cannot arm them, and keep them supplied with ammunition for their arms, we might as well attach ourselves to whatever Power we may consider likely to be 'top dog' in the event of the overthrow of England. We have been very ready to assist her. It might be as well to make sure that we can help ourselves. We don't want uniform factories, or gold lace contractors, but we cannot do without cartridges.

And now we come to the end. The suns rise and set over the grey fields and the blue kopjes out there across the Indian Ocean, and the glorious days of the 'high veldt' are as divinely blue and clear as ever they were for us. The same dirty, yellow-coated men loaf about the streets of the quiet stads and dorps; the same dingy guns still point menacingly half skyward; the same steady rifles still rest over ant heaps and rocks; the same long trains puff slowly over the Karoo towards De Aar and Naauwpoort. But the end of it is in sight. The guns and the rifles will point, and the provision trains crawl about the country for a while longer. In a year or more the rifles will be carried at the 'shoulder' instead of at the 'ready'—in God's own time they will be laid down, and there will come the five-furrowed plough amongst the graves, and the noise of the stamper battery will supersede the noise of the field-battery. For us who have come back, the end is here. Black coat or shirt-sleeves instead of khaki—stock-whip and shear-blade instead of rifle. Cattle or sheep to herd instead of worn-out horses—prospecting drives to dig instead of trenches. Kangaroos to hunt instead of men.

Some of us have 'gone drovin', ' some of us have 'humped bluey'. Most of us have 'roughed it' somewhere in Australia at some time—but none of us as we did in Africa.

And yet there was something about it all that calls you back again—some devilish fascination in the life of war-time that will never leave you without a hankering for more of it. "There is no hunting like the hunting of man! "

The end for us is the drafting-yard, and the farm in the river bend, and the shearing floor, and the stripped saddle of peaceful avocation, and the office. The end for Africa is yet to shape itself. But the days of war, in spite of what he might have thought at the time — in spite of whatever may become of him in the after years — will always return with something of indefinable pleasure in their remembrance to 'Tommy Cornstalk'.

THE END

Lightning Source UK Ltd.
Milton Keynes UK
UKHW010636270521
384471UK00001B/64